What the critics are saying:

"This story touched me on many levels. Doomed love affairs are always sad and uncomfortable, but "the way out" in this particular story was unique and inventive. Love at first sight is always a classic touch and the ending, although not totally unexpected, was still a marvelous resolution. The characters are unique to that particular time period, with the hero not only brave but compassionate and willing to share his feelings with his lady almost from their first meeting and the lady understanding and embracing the new house she finds herself in without trying to change its ways. My compliments to Ms. Kingston on this unique and wonderful story." - *Amy L. Turpin, Timeless Tales Reviews*

"Katherine Kingston makes you laugh and cry with the tale she weaves in RULING PASSION. Her characters come to life and deal with choices of honor and loyalty. The characters of Jeoffrey and Rosalind are sensual and passionate, making you look at chivalry with a whole new perspective. She takes a doomed love and turns it into a triumph. Ms. Kingston will surprise you with twists and turns, giving you the unexpected in a most delightful manner. I was impressed. - *D. Sullivan, Romance Studio*

"This story is well written and believable. You get caught up in the characters and the development of their romance. Honor is a strong theme throughout this tale." - *Sharon M. Bressen, Sensual Romance*

PASSIONS: RULING PASSION
An Ellora's Cave Publication, September 2004

Ellora's Cave Publishing, Inc.
PO Box 787
Hudson, OH 44236-0787

ISBN #1-4199-5022-3

ISBN MS Reader (LIT) ISBN #1-84360-019-6
Other available formats (no ISBNs are assigned):
Adobe (PDF), Rocketbook (RB), Mobipocket (PRC) & HTML

Edited by Christina Brashear
Cover art by Syneca

PASSIONS:
RULING PASSION

Katherine Kingston

Chapter One

An enormous cockroach scurried across the stone floor of the cell.

Lady Rosalind Hamilton shivered as she watched it race toward the shelter of a tiny crevice in the stone wall. She drew around her the thin blanket that failed to deliver any warmth. At least she could see the insect right now, but soon she'd only be able to locate her small roommates by sound. The thin gray light from the single, high, barred window was fading, and the guards provided no candles. A cloudy night meant thick darkness, a blackness so complete it pressed on her body and invaded her soul.

In the depths of the blackest nights, she asked herself why she didn't just accede to Sir William's demands and yield herself to him. But it was also in those soul-searing hours she remembered her father's head rolling on the floor several feet from his body. She saw again her older brother's sightless eyes and the blood soaking his clothes. Heard her mother's screams as William's men dragged her to another room. Her shrieks of pain sank gradually to despairing moans. Then, even those stopped, leaving an empty silence.

Rosalind knew she would likely die here, but better so than give the monster anything of herself. How could he think he would get anything from her but hatred?

Even his efforts to "convince" her to do his will were despicable. He'd tried to bribe her with fine clothes and jewels, exotic foods and sweets, the best accommodations in his keep. When those failed to move her, he went the other way and consigned her to the laundry rooms. She cringed remembering how the other servants, no doubt at Sir William's instigation, gave her the foulest items to wash, slopped and splashed her with rank-smelling water, and once nearly knocked her into one of the caldrons. Her scalded arm had burned for days.

The monster would not have her.

But she didn't want to die in this God-forsaken cell. She'd tried the window, standing on the rickety cot that was the only furnishing. The bars refused to yield to her tugs and pulls. Even her full weight hanging from them hadn't produced so much as a wiggle. Her fingertips were scraped raw from trying to dig around the mortar holding the bars in place. She'd investigated every square inch of the cell for weaknesses and found none. The door was solid wood, six inches thick, with a tiny little window and no flaws or cracks.

Rosalind sat on the cot and prayed. It would take a miracle to free her.

Chapter Two

The corridors of the dungeon echoed the scraping of his men's rushing feet and the prisoners' desperate flight to freedom. Lord Jeoffrey Blaisdell frowned as he strained to decipher another sound he thought he heard.

"Jeoff, come on. We must get out of here. The time grows short!" Sir Philip de Mont Charles demanded.

Lord Jeoffrey held a finger to his lips, over the hood that shrouded his face, and hissed, "Silence." He glared at the speaker, though Philip was, in truth, his closest friend. "There is someone else here."

"The captain of the guard, I should imagine," Philip whispered, his voice muffled by the fabric concealing his features. "Coming to check on the prisoners."

"No, 'tis a woman's voice."

A moment later they both heard a plaintive cry. "Over here. Please."

Jeoffrey looked both ways down the dank, smelly corridor of the dungeon. The call had come from his left. He turned to look the other way. "Are the others all off?" he asked Philip.

"Aye," Philip said. "All but we two."

The female voice captured their attention again. "For pity's sake, help me."

"Go," Jeoffrey said. "Get the others away. Leave my horse, and I shall join you later."

"Jeoff, nay. You will risk all our work. We have everyone we came for. Whoever she is, she's not our task. The captain will be coming to make his rounds in just a few minutes."

"'Tis my problem. Go," Jeoffrey urged him. "Get the others away."

"Your damned sense of chivalry will be the death of us all."

"Only if you do not stop arguing. Now, go!" He put as much force as he could behind the word without raising his voice.

Philip hesitated only another second. "Do not be long," he said, meeting and holding the other man's gaze for a moment.

"I shall be with you anon."

Jeoffrey turned and headed down the corridor. He didn't think the smell—a composite of damp earth, rotted food, and human excrement—could get any worse, but it did the farther along he went.

He stopped and listened. This part of the dungeon couldn't be much used. It was far too quiet. Then the woman's voice called again, "Please, help."

The sound came from a door just ahead and to his left. He peered through the small, high window and saw, dimly, since the cell had no light of its own, a disheveled young woman sitting primly on a rickety cot. The key scraped in the lock as he turned it, making him wince. Then the mechanism gave and he pulled the door open.

Jeoff thrust the torch he carried forward before he entered the small space. The young woman looked up at him, hope warring with apprehension in her expression. She had wide, yearning brown eyes, large and heavily lashed. Their stare went to his heart like a dagger, and he only just kept himself from flinching. This was a danger he didn't need. But he couldn't leave her now. Aside from the glorious eyes, he couldn't tell much about what she might look like beneath the grime and greasy lank hair, but her clothes, though patched and mended, had once been of good quality. The figure filling them was slim but rounded enough to set off a stir in his nether regions. He didn't need that, either, right now.

"I know you took the others out. Please take me with you, too." she begged.

"How much is it worth to you?" he asked, making the words a harsh demand

She gasped. "I don't— A thousand crowns."

He nodded. "Be quiet and come with me."

She hesitated only a moment before grabbing a small bag on the cot next to her and moving toward him.

Jeoffrey led the way down the corridor and up the stone staircase to ground level. He paused when he heard the tromp of heavy boots, rolled the torch on the floor to extinguish it, and drew back into a shadowy niche with the girl pushed in behind him. The heady rush of danger and the feminine hip and breast pressed against his back combined to set his senses aflame and his lower regions alight. A heavyset guard ambled by, which meant the alarm would shortly sound. As soon as the man was out of sight, Jeoffrey pulled the girl with him to a secret door that had been left unlocked for him.

Once they were through, he dragged a huge breath of cool, clean, fresh air into his lungs before turning to make sure the door was secured. In the darkness of early evening he nearly stumbled a couple of times, but finally got to the rock where they had tethered the horses.

His mount calmly chewed grass as he waited. Jeoffrey tossed the girl up into the saddle and mounted behind her. She reeked almost as badly as the dungeon that had been her late abode. He vowed she'd get a bath first thing they arrived at his manor.

Once they were well away, she twisted so she could see his face. "Thank you," she said. "I thought I'd rot forever in that cell."

"I did not do it for thanks," he said. "You promised a thousand crowns for the service. I expect to be paid. I presume you have some family who will be glad of your return."

She sighed. "I fear not. They were all killed when Sir William de Railles took my father's manor."

"You will have an inheritance from them, though."

She didn't answer. After a minute he looked down and realized she was dozing off, leaning against his chest. He sighed and concentrated on keeping the horse to the road, which was lit only by the radiance of the newly risen moon. When the way grew broader and flatter, he increased the pace until he caught up with Philip, his other men and the former captives they'd rescued.

A merry party returned to his manor. He handed the young woman over to a housemaid to be put to bath and bed in that order before he stripped off hood and cloak and joined the others in a late meal and celebration. He served up the best brandy in his cellar in honor of the occasion. Jeoffrey retired in the early hours, well satisfied with the outcome of his mission.

He considered going to see how his last charge was doing. He admitted a desire to know what she looked like cleaned up, since his veins still pulsed with the desire she'd engendered. The slender lines of her figure had been so inviting. The arm he'd wrapped around her had brushed against a soft breast. But he'd best not warm himself with thoughts that would go nowhere. She'd likely buy her way forward and be gone within days.

At first light in the morning several messengers set out, carrying the news of the rescue to various family members of the captives. The young lady still slept, and clearly she needed the rest, so he let her be. Another messenger could be dispatched later for her ransom.

Chapter Three

Rosalind roused but chose not to wake fully just yet. The unaccustomed luxury of a soft bed and clean linens on her scrubbed body felt so delicious she had to revel in it for a while before she would face the problems attendant on her unexpected rescue. But once those thoughts entered her head they wouldn't be chased away again. She couldn't help but consider her situation.

She wasn't in Sir William's dungeon anymore. The fact was both a wonder, coming so unexpectedly as it had, and a quandary, for she'd told her rescuer she could pay him and she'd lied.

She didn't like having lied. It was dishonest and dishonorable, and her father had always stressed to her the importance of dealing honestly with others. It left a sour feeling in her stomach. At the time, though, she simply couldn't face staying another moment in that cell when an offer of rescue was at hand.

He might have taken her anyway, even if she'd admitted she couldn't pay him. She had no way to judge the kind of man Lord Jeoffrey Blaisdell was. She knew him to be strong and brave and clever, just from the fact that he'd managed to make his way into and out of De Railles' dungeon. The rest remained to be seen.

From her brief glimpse by the uncertain light of the torch, she'd been able to see little of the face hidden by a hood with small holes cut out for eyes, nose, and mouth. His form was tall and muscular, and he moved with lithe grace. The body she'd pressed up against while they hid from the guard and then shared a horse had been strong, straight, and hard under leather

13

and linen garments, with an aroma that was enticingly male. And his voice, rough and dark, had made her shiver, not entirely from fear, when he asked her about her family.

His looks mattered naught, though. Nor did the strange effect he had on her. It concerned her more to know what he would do when he learned she couldn't pay him the price they'd agreed upon.

The door creaked, interrupting her unhappy thoughts, and a maid addressed her. "Miss? Ah, so you are awake. I've tea and bread for you. And my lord wishes to see you as soon as you're ready."

Rosalind conceded and sat up on the side of the bed.

An hour and a half later, washed, dressed, fed and groomed, she steeled herself to face Lord Jeoffrey Blaisdell.

The same maid who'd brought her breakfast led the way down a flight of stairs and along two chilly corridors before she stopped at and knocked on a closed door.

The deep voice Rosalind remembered from the previous evening called, "Enter." Shivers crawled up and down her spine.

As she entered, the man rose from a padded chair behind a trestle table bearing a pair of quills, an inkwell and a stack of papers. He was bigger than she'd remembered, almost a full head taller than herself. A plain green tunic over a white shirt draped from broad shoulders along a strong chest. His narrow waist was circled by a wide leather belt. Tan hose clung to long, lean, muscular legs.

His face drew her attention and held it. Prominent cheekbones and the brightest, most penetrating gray eyes she'd ever seen dominated lean, finely shaped features. The stern, almost harsh, expression just emphasized the clean, hard lines of the handsome visage. Wavy blond hair was drawn back and caught in a leather thong at his nape.

Her breath caught in her throat and her heart pounded against the constraints of her chest. He was both the most beautiful and the most heart-stoppingly male creature she'd ever seen in her life. Terror warred with fascination as she watched him, waiting for the question she dreaded.

He studied her in silence for a while, and she could judge nothing from his expression. When he spoke there was little emotion to be read in his tone either, despite the complimentary words, "You've cleaned up more spectacularly than I expected."

"My lord…" She didn't know how to react to that. "Thank you."

He nodded off-handedly. "I expect there's a man somewhere who'd give a great deal for your return."

She drew a long breath and chewed at her lip before she answered, "I fear not, my lord."

"You are not married, or at least betrothed?"

"Nay."

"Why not? Who is your family, by the way? Your name? I presume you have been informed that I'm Jeoffrey Blaisdell."

"Aye, my lord. I am Lady Rosalind Hamilton. My father was the Earl of Highwaith until Sir William de Railles took Highwaith and slaughtered my family."

"But he spared you."

"He wanted me."

"For wife?"

"Aye."

"I'm not surprised. He threw you in his dungeon when you refused his suit."

She drew a deep breath to control the fury that roused every time she remembered. "He massacred my entire family. I'd as soon mate with his horse."

A grin crooked one corner of Lord Jeoffrey's mouth, revealing a wickedly attractive groove in his cheek. "A damned uncomfortable coupling I should imagine."

She blushed but answered calmly, "The dungeon was not commodious either."

"But you are now free of it." The grin faded and his face took on the harsh cast again. "Which brings us again to the question of payment. Since you've no family and no betrothed to reimburse me for my rescue efforts, I presume you will draw on your own personal fortune."

She kept her back straight and her head high. "My lord, about the payment... I fear I cannot pay quite as much as I offered last night. Desperation made me forget how much diminished my personal resources are."

One handsome blond eyebrow crooked. "How much do you believe you can offer?"

"How much do you normally ask in these cases?"

"It depends on the value of the persons to those who wish their return."

"And how much do you suppose I should be worth to myself?"

"Only you can truly answer that, my lady. But I should regard you as nearly priceless, were you mine."

"Indeed that is how I view myself. Priceless."

He saw the trap and avoided it. "Yet I fear business and my reputation demand we put a price on your rescue," he said. "I could accept eight hundred crowns."

She gasped. "Eight hundred?"

"I realize it greatly undervalues you, my lady, but we must be realistic."

"Realistic," she repeated. "Nay."

"Nay?" he asked. "Nay, it's not realistic, or nay, you will not pay?"

She drew herself up straight. "Both. It's not realistic. And I cannot pay it."

"How much might you offer, then?"

She had to take a deep breath. "I cannot pay you anything in gold."

The same blond eyebrows rose. The shiver that went down her spine this time held an element of fear as well as admiration.

"Last night you claimed you could," he said.

"I was desperate to be free of that cell," she admitted. "But I shall pay you in any way I can."

A cold light sparkled in the narrowed gray eyes. "Money is the coin of exchange I deal in. That is what you promised me last night."

"And I thought you an honorable man last night," she countered. "One who would understand a woman's desperation. One who could value a human life over any amount of money."

His expression didn't change. "I regret, my lady, I do not have the luxury of such sentimentalities. The money I earn from risking my life and those of the men who serve me supports my estate, the people who work on it, myself, and my king."

Rosalind bit her lip briefly and drew in a long, hard breath. "I would willingly pay you with my service."

He looked her up and down. "What kind of service can you offer, my lady?"

She eyed the papers on his desk. "I can read, write and cipher. My father and mother relied on my skills in managing the household."

"But I already have people performing those duties."

"I can cook," she offered desperately.

"Not as well as my present cook, I'd warrant."

"Then what would you have from me?"

He drew a deep breath and let it escape slowly as he considered. "If you cannot offer the money you promised, there's only one other thing I might accept from you. Your personal service. One night and a day only. I believe it a fair bargain. Freeing you from the dungeon for one day of your time." He looked at her. "Are you yet a maiden?"

"I am, my lord."

"Sir William did not...force you?"

"Nay, he did not. He yet believed he could gain my agreement. I doubt not he would have come around to taking me by force ere long."

"Think you not, then, that a day of your person, given voluntarily, would compensate for saving your from that fate?"

Rosalind hesitated. The bargain might be a fair one, but it put her future in jeopardy. If it were known, she'd have great difficulty making any advantageous marriage. Of course, she was now without friends, family, lands or dowry. Her odds of any marriage at all were virtually nil. And if she chose to take the veil, her status as maiden would be of little consequence.

"Perhaps. Should I refuse, would you return me to Sir William's dungeon?"

He stared at her, the light in the gray eyes hard, almost cutting in its intensity. "Nay, lady, that I wouldn't. But I would be forced to ask you to remove yourself from my estates immediately."

"I see. And should I agree to your proposal, what would be my position tomorrow?"

"Ah, now that is yet to be seen. But I would offer you my promise of whatever assistance was in my power in finding an appropriate refuge." His lips and eyes narrowed as another thought occurred to him. "But, of course, we have to deal with the fact of your lie as well."

"'Deal with', my lord?"

"You lied when you promised to pay me for taking you from the dungeon. I do not countenance lies in my household or from those I do business with. I can do nothing at all for you until that has been set straight."

Her heartbeat kicked up again and her chest got tight. A trickle of perspiration slid down between her breasts, tickling as it went. "Set straight, my lord?"

"Set straight," he repeated. "The error atoned for."

"And what, in your view, would be the proper atonement for my lies?"

"In this household, the usual penalty for lying about an important matter is a dozen cuts with the birch."

Rosalind felt the blood rising in a flush on her face, and her chest, already tight, nearly closed down completely. Shock made her feel disoriented and off-balance, but she straightened her back, refusing to give in to it. "But, my lord, I'm a lady. Surely that makes a difference."

"Not in my home. Discipline is applied equally to lord, lady, cook, housekeeper, all the way down to the lowest scullery maid. Justice and fairness prevail here."

"Does that include yourself, my lord?"

"I've taken my stripes when I've failed in my duties," he answered.

Rosalind searched for a chair to settle in. Shock and fear made her light-headed. This wasn't at all what she'd expected. The seat she found was hard and straight, providing no comfort but some support.

"You, my lord?" she asked faintly.

"You believe me not?" He drew a breath and bellowed, "Ferris!"

Moments later an elderly man opened the door and walked in. "My lord?" he said.

"Ferris, this is Lady Rosalind. Tell the lady what happens in this household when someone is found to have lied."

"About a serious matter, my lord?"

"About a serious matter," he confirmed.

The man turned to Rosalind. "The usual punishment is a dozen strokes with the rod, my lady."

"And if the lord of the household was found to have lied?" Lord Jeoffrey prompted.

The man's faded blue eyes flicked to his master. "He would get a dozen strokes."

"Has it ever happened?"

The man's brow crinkled as he thought. "I recall not you've ever been accused of lying, my lord. But there was the time a few months back when you accused Martine of lying and punished her for it, and it turned out you had been mistaken."

"Indeed," Lord Jeoffrey said. "What chanced then?"

"You took two dozen strokes," the man said. "Took them quite well, I must say, my lord."

"Thank you, Ferris," Lord Jeoffrey said. "That's all."

The man nodded, bowed to his master and to Rosalind, and left.

She just stared at him, more stunned than she'd ever been in her life, more astonished even than when Sir William demanded she cede herself to him.

Lord Jeoffrey looked to Rosalind again. "I run a strict and orderly household, but I strive for fairness. No matter what the rank of those committing them, wicked deeds are punished." His bright, sharp gaze seemed to bore into her.

"And if I decline to accept this?"

"I told you earlier. You're to leave my premises immediately. From there on your fate is no longer my concern."

"Would you at least provide me an escort to the nearest convent?"

"Nay, lady. I would not."

"You wouldn't help me at all?"

"One who would make a promise she knew she couldn't keep and then refuse to accept the consequences of the deed is not such a person as I would deem worthy of my assistance."

Rosalind settled back, struggling to push aside her emotions so she could consider her choices rationally. It wasn't easily done, however. And in making the attempt she discovered another, unexpected emotion forming: admiration for Lord Jeoffrey and a desire for his good regard. She couldn't help but be drawn to his strength and good looks. Even more though, here was a man in whom bold courage and daring appeared to be mixed with a fundamentally fair and honorable nature. Under other circumstances he'd be exactly the sort of man she would wish to join herself with.

His demands of her were no more than just by his own code. She had lied to him. Had a servant done so in her own household she'd have ordered a similar punishment without a second thought. But as the daughter of the lord, she'd always been exempt from such justice. Her father had adored his daughters and could hardly bear even to raise his voice to them when they behaved in unacceptable ways. She'd certainly never been subject to anything as severe as the penalty he proposed. But she had lied to him, and allowed him to risk his life thinking she could make it worth his effort. An effort he indicated he put forth to help support his lands and people. She couldn't convince herself she didn't deserve chastisement.

She had a real choice in the matter, though. It would challenge her to make her way cross country to the nearest convent while avoiding Sir William's troops, roving marauders, robbers, and other natural perils; but she considered herself resourceful enough to do it. Had she thought him unreasonable or unjust, she'd attempt it without a second thought. Well, maybe a small regret for what might have been.

But he wasn't unfair. Nor was his price all that high, measured against her probable future had he left her in the dungeon.

And then there was the man himself. It shouldn't weigh in her decision that he was the most attractive man she'd ever met. It shouldn't, but it did. In all likelihood, there would be no future with him beyond the night and day he asked, even if she agreed to his terms. But if he kept his promise, there would be some kind of life ahead for her, and perhaps even a chance for a reasonable marriage.

The truth was she didn't want to commit herself to the convent and the veil. She felt no call from God toward that life. Meeting Lord Jeoffrey, weighing her reaction to him made her realize that more strongly then ever. She admired the man, and she wanted his good regard. Wanted it enough to take some risk with her future, as well as a punishment she probably deserved.

She looked up again at the man who sat watching her, waiting patiently for the outcome of her deliberations. If he cared which way she chose, nothing of it showed on his face.

Rosalind drew a deep breath and cleared her throat before answering him. "I agree to your terms."

His expression didn't change as he watched her silently for a moment, then asked, "Why?"

"Why did I agree?" She rubbed together hands suddenly gone cold and shaky. "Because it's right. I was dishonest with you and I want to set it right."

"And because you have no alternative?"

"I could make my way to the nearest convent on my own should I feel it the right thing to do."

"You're quite sure." His tone mixed astonishment with an amusement that didn't show on his face.

"Aye."

"Then I honor you for the decision you've made."

"May I ask a favor then?"

"Ask, and I'll honor it if I can."

"Can we do it quickly? Have it over?"

"Normally punishment sessions are held after dinner in the great hall. Since you're not a member of this household, yours will be administered privately, in my chambers. We'll begin the time of your payment to me immediately thereafter." He looked down at his desk. "There's work I must finish before I can take the time for you. When it's done, I'll summon you."

She couldn't keep her voice from quavering when she said, "As you will, my lord."

He nodded at her, turning his attention once again to the papers before him.

Chapter Four

Rosalind retreated to the bedchamber she'd occupied the previous night. Moments later a serving girl knocked on the door and handed her a bundle of clothing.

"My lord requested this be delivered to you. He asked that you assume the garments immediately. I'm to help you out of your current things, but he said you could see to getting into these on your own."

The girl helped unfasten the borrowed garments Rosalind currently wore, then she departed. The clothing delivered proved to be nothing more than a simple shift that went on over the head and draped straight down from her shoulders to her ankles. A warmer, more enveloping robe accompanied it. A note included in the bundle indicated she was to wear nothing but these garments alone when she presented herself at his summons.

She removed the overdress, undershift and hose she'd been offered that morning, put on the plain shift and robe, then seated herself on the side of the bed. Terror nearly overwhelmed her as she waited. She wanted to run from what she faced or chew her fingernails down to the quick. Time dragged almost unbearably as she attempted to prepare herself for what was to come. After what seemed a very long wait, a knock sounded on the door. The same serving girl entered bringing a lunch tray and another message.

"My lord said to convey his regret for the delay to you. A messenger has arrived concerning a matter that requires his urgent attention. He said, too, it would likely be midafternoon before he could attend to your needs, and he begged your patience."

So she waited for another endless, agonizing stretch of time, until the knock came as the light was beginning to fade from the sky outside her window. A different girl entered at her bidding and informed her Lord Jeoffrey was now prepared to accommodate her. The girl led the way down several corridors and up a flight of stairs to the lord's private chambers.

Lord Jeoffrey himself opened the door to them, thanked the girl and sent her away, then conducted Rosalind into a large, comfortable room. A warm, welcoming fire crackled at one end, while a sumptuous bed, canopied and curtained, stood at the other. A table and chair were pushed to one wall of the room to make way for a long padded bench sitting in the middle. Lying beside it were several bundles of twigs lashed together into well-branched, wicked-looking rods.

She stumbled and almost fell against him, but he steadied her with warm, strong hands on her arms.

"Keep up your courage," he exhorted her. "It'll be over ere long."

"You won't be too hard on me, please?" She hated begging, but staring at the instruments of her punishment and thinking of the damage they could do sapped her nerve.

"You'll get exactly what you've earned," he promised, which didn't reassure her at all. "Come, now."

He requested she remove the outer robe and she did so, then stood before him in nothing but the shift. His gaze ran up and down her body, and for a moment something hot and yearning and hungry lit his face. He suppressed it, reached out to take her arm, guided her to the bench, and helped her lie on it, face down.

"Normally I'd have someone hold you," he said. "But since we're doing this privately, I'm going to fasten you down. It's too much to ask a person to keep themselves still and not try to get up or protect themselves during such a punishment."

Her heart began pounding even harder and her breath became a pant as her wrists were tied with soft lengths of cloth to the legs of the bench just beyond her head. Her fear grew when he raised her shift, pulling it up over her legs and derriere, exposing her from the waist down to the cool air and his hot view.

"My lord!" she protested. "It isn't seemly!"

He laughed. "You forget the rest of our bargain. The payment you're offering me. I'll shortly be seeing even more of your body, so fret it not."

"Do you thus punish everyone in your household?" she asked.

"In general I feel punishment is most effective on bare flesh. And I think the act of unclothing oneself to receive discipline is a salutary reminder. I make exceptions in some cases where it seems warranted. I see no such circumstances here."

A length of cloth went around her waist, over the bunched material of the drawn-up shift and under the bench so that it held her in place on the bench and kept the garment from sliding back down. Finally, cloths wound around her ankles were fastened to the other legs of the bench.

Fear escalated to the point of nearly choking her, but oddly, mixed with it was a strange lacing of excitement and satisfaction. At some level she trusted that Lord Jeoffrey might cause her pain, but he wouldn't injure her or hurt her any more than was due for her lie. And in some peculiar part of her mind she was pleased he cared enough to do this for her. She wanted to give this to him. She wanted to show him her sense of honor matched his own, even to accepting discipline she knew would be painful. She would never have guessed it could be so and would have stridently denied it had anyone suggested such a thing to her.

Every other thought but fear fled her mind when she heard the rustle of the twigs as he picked up the birch rod. She shut her eyes and tensed her muscles in expectation of the first stroke and resolved to bear it as bravely as she could. No cries, moans or pleas would escape her lips if she could help it.

The branches made a whispering hiss as they whipped through the air and emitted a series of closely-spaced, sharp cracks when they struck her flesh.

The shock of impact barely preceded the explosion of burning pain fired by the twigs clawing into her flesh. She jerked as far as the bindings would allow. However much she'd tried to anticipate the pain of the whipping, nothing could have prepared her for the rush of agony that centered in her bottom and spread in a hideous burn through every nerve and muscle of her body. Despite her resolve, she couldn't suppress a whimper. It was terrible: fierce and burning. Worst of all, she suspected he hadn't used anything like all the force of his arm behind that cut.

Eleven more to go. She couldn't take it. She'd die of the pain long before they reached a dozen.

The fiery sting had settled down to a more bearable itchy burn when she heard the ominous hiss signaling the imminence of another lash. It landed even harder than the previous one, spreading a corrosive fire across her derriere. She jerked more this time and struggled against the bindings holding her in place. A soft, low moan escaped as she tensed against the red-hot sting.

Again and again the birch rod printed ribbons of fire on her bottom. Between each lash he waited for some time, letting the pain of the previous stroke rise, crest and begin to settle before delivering the next. The third one set her moaning again and bouncing up and down as far as she could, but the fourth was so agonizing it drew a shallow scream and the pleas she'd hoped wouldn't be dragged from her.

"Please," she begged. "I can't bear it. I can't. Please stop. I'll never lie again. I promise. Never." The entreaties ended in another shrill squeal when the birch cut again, lower down, so that some of the twigs clawed at her upper thighs.

She sobbed and moaned. Her hands clutched at the legs of the bench, squeezing as hard as she could while her body heaved and jerked so hard the cloth binding around her waist pinched. "Oh, my lord, my lord," she groaned as the fire engulfed her bottom and scraped along her skin to every extremity.

The next lash was full across the backs of her thighs, not as hard as the previous cut, but still with enough force to bury the ends of the twigs deep into her flesh where they printed more agonizing welts.

"Oh my lord, I can't stand it," she wailed. "It's killing me." Her bottom throbbed horribly, streaks of fire smoldering on her flesh. Her breath came on a series of short, hard sobs and she desperately wanted to rub the stinging areas.

The next cut laid down additional lines of fire, engulfing her in a pain unlike anything she'd ever experienced before in her life. She'd lost count of the strokes and had no idea how many more were yet to come, but she felt sure she couldn't stand even one more. It would surely kill her.

Another lash sent the wicked twigs raking across her derriere again, biting at welts already there and laying down new ones. She screamed shrilly and then burst into loud sobs.

So distracted was she by the engulfing pain, she was stunned when the next stroke on her body didn't come from the birch rod, but was a gentle brush of Lord Jeoffrey's hand across her cheek. She opened her eyes and met his. The lord knelt on the floor beside her, leaning over and watching her, his face serious and worried.

"Is it over?" she asked.

"There are four strokes remaining. I was worried about you." He brushed her cheek again and the contrast between the gentleness of his fingers and the harsh bite of the rod made her heart flutter. "You've never been punished this way before. I'm afraid it might be too much for you. Can you handle four more?"

Her throbbing derriere demanded she say no. She met his worried gray eyes. The expression on his face, the concern showing there as well as the respect for her confirmed her suspicions that beneath the sternness lurked a kind and caring man. A man she could admire and respect. A man whose respect and admiration she wanted. Wanted badly.

"I can handle it," she said, fighting to get the words past her fear.

He smiled at her. The way it lit his face warmed her soul and soothed some of the ache in her flaming bottom. He leaned closer and his lips brushed hers, stopped and came back to linger. His tongue brushed gently across her bottom lip and her body ignited in flames, a torch set alight by the contact.

The heat and pain of her whipped derriere fed another sort of heat that settled in her nether regions. Every inch of her skin felt super-sensitized, awake to the least touch. Her female parts swelled, moistened in a way she'd never experienced before and a yearning roused, a need that wanted something more to complete it. She didn't know exactly what it was but suspected Lord Jeoffrey could supply it, should he choose.

Had she not been fastened so securely to the bench, she'd have moved to press herself against him, to investigate the strange new feelings his touch roused in her. Instead she fluttered her lips and parted them to provide entrance to his tongue. When it slipped into the opening she offered, the flames flared brighter and hotter. A desperate, needy wanting roused and she welcomed the hot intrusion of his tongue, moaning deep in her throat when he explored the sensitive walls of her mouth and wiped across her teeth.

Their tongues danced and twined together in a way that set her blood pounding in its course. No man had ever done this to her. She couldn't imagine ever letting any other man of her acquaintance do something so intimate and exciting.

When he carefully broke the suction and pulled his mouth away from hers, she felt bereft and abandoned. He swept a caressing finger over her lips as he smiled at her again and said, "More soon, my dear. Be brave now, while we finish up your discipline so we can get to more pleasant activities."

He stood up and moved back. She closed her eyes after she saw him pick up a fresh rod from the floor and shake it out.

She might harbor a small hope that the kiss would induce some mercy, but she didn't expect it and didn't get it. In fact, the next lash was the cruelest yet, as the fresh rod whipped across her bottom with more force than he'd previously used. Her scream hurt her throat and shocked her with its agonizing protest.

One small concession she did gain: the next three strokes followed in more rapid succession. Those strokes tortured her with an agony she'd never have thought she could bear. But oddly, they also fed that other flame, the one that had roused in her loins when he'd kissed her. As the blaze in her bottom and thighs tormented her, so too did the flames of need and wanting sing in her blood until she was awash in sensation to the point of becoming light-headed.

One last lightning bolt of blinding pain struck. She screamed and was so wrought-up she couldn't stop screaming even when she felt hands on her face, brushing tears off her damp cheeks.

"Shhh," Lord Jeoffrey hushed her. "It's over now. All over. Please calm down."

He brushed her hair back and smoothed it, running gentle fingers into it to hold her. Her shrieks settled to a whimpering that didn't stop until his lips came down over hers. In one stunning shift, she moved from the hell of torturous pain to the bliss of his kiss feeding the rampaging fire of need singing through her.

It went on and on until she lost track of time and place and situation. Her awareness narrowed to her body and the man beside her. She murmured a protest when his lips finally left hers and he stood up again. He unfastened the bindings and helped her up. She was stiff and the pain in her bottom flared into renewed sting as she moved. He grabbed her when she wavered and lifted her into his arms. Holding her carefully against his chest, he moved across the room to the immense bed, pushed the curtains aside, and sat on the side of it, still cradling her. With his legs spread wide, her derriere slid down between them so that no pressure was put on it.

Strong arms held her firmly against his chest. For a moment she just rested there, listening to the strong, reassuring thud of his heart below her right ear. When he pressed a thumb under her chin to tilt her head back, she yielded and met the bright gaze of his gray eyes.

His finger moved up her face to flick away the tears still streaking her cheeks. His mouth twisted into pain and he leaned forward to rest his forehead against her temple.

"I'm sorry," he said.

"Sorry for what? That you punished me? Why be sorry when you and I both know it was right and due?"

"Sorry you had to suffer so. Sorry mine was the hand that made you scream."

"I'm not," she said.

Astonishment spread over the face he lifted so that he could meet her eyes.

"I'm pleased you have such a strong sense of honor you wouldn't let me get away with lying to you," she said. "I rejoice that if I had to be punished for it, the hand doing it was yours."

"You wanted to be punished?" he asked.

"Nay, my lord. And most certainly I didn't enjoy it. But it was right and I needed it."

His face plunged toward her again and his lips clamped on her mouth. She opened to him and his tongue roved the insides of her cheeks and gums. No longer constrained, she wrapped her arms around his chest and pressed closer to him. The feel of his solid muscle and the manly scent of his skin made her nearly dizzy. The kiss went on and on until her loins and her bottom both throbbed in unison with her pounding pulse. Something hard and probing poked at her hip and she moved against it.

Pleasure surged through her when he groaned and rubbed a big hand up and down her back. Tearing his mouth from hers, he kissed his way to her ear and then down along the side of her neck, sucking and nipping at the tender flesh as he went. She moaned in turn. One of his arms still circled her back and supported her. The other hand moved around to the front of her shift and found the neat handful of a breast. He cupped it in his palm while his fingers sought the tip. The soft flesh hardened in welcome of the touch.

Her head fell back a little when new waves of pleasure radiated from her nipple as he caressed it and pinched it lightly. He moved to the other breast and played with it, too. She squealed in surprise and delight when his lips replaced his fingers on her nipple and he tongued it through the cloth of her shift, sucking and nipping lightly.

"Oh, my lord, my lord," she moaned as a pleasure just as intense as the pain she'd suffered only minutes before flooded her being to the point where she doubted her body could contain it.

With his mouth still clinging to her breast, he reached down and grabbed the bottom edge of the shift. He released her nipple long enough to tug the garment up and over her head, leaving her completely naked to his gaze. It should have embarrassed her, but instead she just felt a warm excitement about it.

"Beautiful," he murmured as his gaze roved over her revealed charms. "You're so beautiful."

He dipped his head to take another mouthful of breast and taste the naked bud. The shards of pleasure that exploded from it ripped through her gut and her loins, making her moan loudly again. She'd never felt anything so exciting and rapturous in her life. She'd never dreamed such pleasure could exist.

His free hand began an exploration of the rest of her body, traveling down her side, stroking her belly, moving lower, then bypassing the triangle below to brush her hip and thigh. Warm, exciting tingles followed upon his touch. When his fingers moved toward the flesh of her inner thigh, the pleasure grew into a demanding tension. She needed, wanted something without knowing exactly what it was.

One thing she did know she wanted: the feel of his skin. She had to work her hands down and under the shirt he wore, then let them travel upwards to revel in the feel of his hair-roughened chest. Solid muscles responded with gentle quivers to her exploration. He jumped and exclaimed when her fingers brushed over one of his nipples.

He stood up abruptly, turned, and lowered her gently to the bed, setting her on her side. Before he lay down next to her, he pulled tunic and shirt over his head. She sucked in a hard breath at the sight of his fine, broad shoulders and the strong, elegant muscles of his chest.

"Roll over on your stomach," he said.

She hesitated for a second, then did as he asked. His hands were gentle on her back, rubbing just hard enough to relax her, kneading the skin. When they moved down over her sore, welted buttocks, his fingers gentled more and caressed just enough to relieve some of the remaining ache.

"Am I bleeding?" she asked.

"Nay, lady," he said, "Though you'll have some mild bruises."

"I'm amazed. It felt as though the rod cut me to ribbons."

"It feels that way," he agreed. "But it's not the case."

His hands slid lower, brushing down along the backs of her thighs and coming up inside them. She gasped and tensed as his fingers left trails of fire along the super-sensitive skin. When they approached the apex of the triangle, they stilled for a moment, then one finger hesitantly brushed her mound.

She squealed as the touch went through her like a charge of energy, leaving her jerking and quivering. He continued stroking the insides of her thighs, his fingers occasionally straying to the magic area where each contact was a revelation of new pleasure. A tension of need and wanting was building within her.

Something cool and a little damp touched her derriere at one of the sore spots. His lips stroked over the welt and then his tongue ran along it. The touch rasped, but the icy burn of it made her suck in air so hard she could only breathe in sharp pants.

"My lord!" she gasped, a little shocked, entirely grateful.

He licked along each line of fire the birch had raised, soothing the pain, building her need and yearning until she was sure she couldn't contain it much longer.

"Can you roll over?" he asked.

She nodded. Her sore bottom protested the contact with the bed linen for a moment then subsided. Oddly, the remaining sting actually fed the yearning tension and seemed to magnify the pleasure of each touch of his hand on her skin.

Lying on her back had the added benefit of letting her see him as he paid homage to her body. Watching the pleasure light his face, it suddenly struck her what an enormous change had happened in her life in the space of twenty-four hours. At the same time the previous day she'd been languishing in Sir William's dungeon, wondering if she would eventually accede to his demand. Now here she was, freely offering her body to a man she'd barely known existed before he took her out of the cell.

Though she did so in payment of her debt to him, she nonetheless found it hard to resist the appeal of him. The attractive exterior drew her, but she admired also his honor, kindness, fairness, and sense of humor. This might be the most right and possibly the most perfect thing she'd ever experienced.

Tomorrow she'd have to consider her future, and without question this night would have a huge influence on it, probably in a negative way. She'd be a used woman, ruined in the eyes of many. But she'd also have known a pleasure she'd never guessed could exist, at the hands of a man unlike any she'd ever known. Whatever happened, she wouldn't regret this night's work, couldn't regret what she'd learned.

He stood upright by the side of the bed, and she ran her eyes up and down his body while he studied hers. Below his beautiful, muscular chest with its flat, brown nipples, the little dip of his belly button drew her eyes further down to the bulge straining his breeches to the limits of the fabric. Possessed suddenly of a wild curiosity, she grabbed and tugged the laces until the bow pulled open and the loosened garment slid down his lean hips.

His cock looked enormous to her. Freed from confinement, it jutted proudly from his body, as long as her hand, as thick as her wrist. Watching his face to be sure she didn't offend him, she reached tentatively to touch it. He sucked in a sharp breath and his face screwed up in a wince of pleasure when she ran the tip of her finger across the bulbous end. She was shocked by how soft and silky the skin felt.

He tolerated her fascinated exploration for another minute or two, then moved until she had to drop her hand. He knelt on the bed at her side and dipped his head to her breasts again. She jerked in stunned delight as he leaned over to run a rasping tongue around her hardened nipple.

Switching from one to the other, he sucked, nipped, swiped the tip with his tongue and rolled it gently between his teeth. His hand ran down her belly to find the hollow between her legs. He parted her outer folds to find the most sensitive places within. The two-pronged assault on her body sent waves of excitement through her and wound her tighter and tighter, like a metal coil pressed down.

His caresses grew faster and harder until she felt the world drop away. Then suddenly the pleasure rose to even greater heights and her body arched in sudden, rapturous release of the tension. Wave on wave of ecstasy coursed through her as she bucked and bounced with breath-stealing pleasure. For a moment out of time she drifted on waves of joy that gradually subsided, leaving her floating comfortably in a place of wondrous peace.

She looked up at him, watching the way his gray eyes glowed with pleasure and pride. She reached up to touch his strong jaw and run her fingers through the loosened blond hair that hung around his shoulders. He leaned forward and kissed her again. Her heart melted in his embrace and a new and different need roused. She wanted more from him. Wanted more for him. Wanted more of him.

He moved to position himself between her legs, weight balanced on his hands as stretched himself out over her. There he hesitated.

"It may be difficult for you," he warned. "It being your first time."

"All will be well, my lord," she said, wrapping her arms around his neck to pull him closer.

He nodded, positioned himself carefully and then thrust forward and into her. When he met the barrier of her maidenhead, he pushed forcefully through it.

Rosalind gasped at the pain and tensed her body. Lord Jeoffrey stopped and held himself still, giving her time to adjust to his invasion. When the burn subsided a bit, she nodded for him to continue. Still he moved cautiously, retreating, pushing forward, waiting for her to accommodate him, all the time watching her face for any sign it was too much. Finally she began to relax, though it still burned. Even with that discomfort, the briefly appeased hunger began to rouse again and she welcomed the movement of him within her. He plunged up and down.

"You're so hot, so tight!" He sounded amazed and delighted, strained and awed. "So beautiful." He lowered his face to hers and kissed her while pumping into her.

She began moving with him, against him and then away, in rhythm with his rocking. His hard body grew even more tense. The motion increased to a nearly frantic pace, but she felt the heat and the need growing again, building, tautening, until she couldn't hold it anymore and she cried out as the shocking spasms rolled through and over her again.

At nearly the same time, he too emitted a sound like a roar, and his face screwed into a mask of agonized pleasure. His hard, gasping breaths testified to the extent of his effort and the pleasure of the reward as he held himself buried deep within her. Moments later, he carefully let himself down until he stretched out on top of her, still maintaining most of his weight on his elbows, but with their bodies touching from chin to knees.

He sighed long and deep as he rested against her. They lay that way, too limp to move, for some time. For Rosalind, peace and contentment saturated her being as she held onto the man. To be so close to another person, to experience so much pleasure and take almost as much joy in giving the equivalent, was a wonder to savor.

Eventually, he rolled off but settled at her side, pulling her against him. She rested her head on his shoulder. They lay quietly together for a while. He sighed and wrapped his arms even tighter around her. One hand crept to her breast and stroked it lightly. His touch was more soothing and comforting than arousing.

"Lady Rosalind," he said. "You are an amazing lady. You could make me begin to wish for what might never be." The words rumbled in his chest.

"What might that be, Lord Jeoffrey?" she asked.

He drew a long breath before he answered. "You make a man feel as though he owns the world and holds it in his hands. Some man will be exceedingly fortunate to have your company lifelong. It cannot be me, however."

"Because I have no lands or dowry?"

"It is not just as I would will," he said. "But what my obligations to my people demand. I do not have lands enough to support my people. I do other work when I can, but it is not dependable enough. I would secure the survival of all my people through a mating of lands or fortunes."

"Always there are obligations to others. Have we no obligations to ourselves?"

"Not for our own happiness," he answered. "Not when others rely on us for all their safety and well-being."

She had no answer for that. While she considered his words, she felt his breath soften as he dozed off. She followed him shortly.

Chapter Five

A tap at the door woke them. The darkness beyond the window showed night had fallen. They'd only slept for a short time. Jeoffrey reached up and pulled the bed curtains closed around them, then called, "Come."

Still in a pleasant haze of sleep and satiation, Rosalind didn't hear much of the conversation that ensued as he poked his head outside the bed curtains to speak with the newcomers. Moments later she heard servants coming and going, pots clattering, pans banging, and the splashing of water being poured from one container to another. It went on for quite a long time. After a while, silence reigned.

Lord Jeoffrey climbed out of the bed, turned back, slid his arms under her and carried her across the room.

"A bath will help soothe your aches," he said, setting her down beside the most enormous hip bath she'd ever seen. Since she had no clothes to shed, he immediately helped her in. The water was hot and cradled her in its steaming glory. She understood the size of the tub when Jeoffrey stepped into it with her and settled himself facing her.

"My second bath in as many days," she said, resting her head against the edge of the tub while the heat penetrated her skin and relaxed her sinews.

"Tis a pleasant habit." He reached over the side of the tub to a small table where a flagon of wine stood beside two cups. His legs touched alongside hers as he moved and poured a measure of liquid into each cup. Rosalind admired the play of strong muscles in his shoulders as he leaned away from her. He turned and handed one of the cups to her, then held his own up, extended toward her. "What shall we drink to?"

Rosalind remembered happier days when her father had made such toasts before the start of a feast. "The usual are things like long life, health, happiness, success."

He cocked his head, waiting for her to continue.

She thought about her childhood and where she was now. Just a few years ago she had felt so safe, so secure in her future. Never would she have anticipated what life would bring her to. She sighed and leaned back against the side of the tub. "I cannot think of anything worth toasting."

"You're alive and no longer in a dungeon," he suggested gently.

"But with an uncertain future."

"Certainty is given to none of us," he said. "We take what we are given and do what can be done with it."

"Then shall we drink to that?" she asked. "To an uncertain future and whatever opportunities it may offer."

A smile spread across his face, lighting the stern features with an unexpected joy. "To opportunities," he agreed and took a long swallow of the wine.

Rosalind straightened up and tried to copy his action, but was surprised by the unexpected burn of it going down and nearly choked.

"Take care," he warned, a trifle late. "Bedwell's brew is more potent than most people expect."

"That it is," she said, staring into the cup, though nothing about the red liquid could serve warning as to how it would burn in the mouth. "But it feels warm all the way down."

She looked up and surprised him staring very hard at her. She watched the intent way his eyes studied her, then let her gaze slip down along his straight nose, the mouth set in uncompromising lines, the firm chin, to the broad, solidly muscled shoulders. The strength and power in the man made her feel small, helpless, frightened.

"Your eyes appear to change color," he said. "Earlier I would have sworn they were brown, but now they look more greenish."

"It has been remarked on before."

He raised the cup and extended it. "I'll drink to your changeable eyes." He took a long sip from the cup.

Hesitantly she held out her cup in turn. "And I'll drink to your eyes—the color of the clouds that precede snow on a winter day." She sipped her wine and waited to see how he would react.

His expression lightened and brightened at her response. "And I'll drink to your hair, neither red nor brown, exactly; the color of some leaves in October," he added, suiting action to his words as he finished.

"And I'll drink to your hair, the yellow of the buttercups in the field."

He frowned wryly. "I know not that I like being compared to a flower."

"'Tis the only thing about you I would compare to so meek and mild a thing."

"Then perhaps I'll allow it," he said. "To your nose, as delicate and graceful as the cup of a daffodil and to the freckles across it and your cheeks like the speckling of dew on the grass."

"Those freckles were my mother's despair." For a moment the memory brought sadness, but he splashed a bit of water in her direction and she let it go. "Your nose, my lord, is anything but delicate, but I drink to the strength and length of it, which reminds me of a guard tower on a castle wall."

He smiled at that and tipped his cup again. "Your lips, my lady, are the soft pink of the earliest spring rosebuds."

She sipped from her own cup and then responded in kind. "To your chin, my lord, which is like the jutting prow of a ship set to sail."

"Have you seen such a ship, my lady?"

"Once. I accompanied my family to France when I was small. The ship made a great impression on me. I should like to set sail on one again sometime."

"Perhaps it will be so for you."

"Perhaps," she agreed.

"In the meantime, I drink to your white shoulders like shapely cliffs and your breasts…to what shall I compare your breasts? Such perfection of form and feel and taste? Perhaps like cook's egg pudding when it comes forth perfect from the mold."

The wine and the heat and the man combined to make her head swim in a pleasantly relaxed way. She let her gaze skim down his form. "And I, my lord, drink to your shoulders, strong as cliffs overlooking the sea; and to your cock, strong, jutting lance that it is, set to penetrate, to bring both pain and ecstasy."

When his arms wrapped around her and his lips locked against hers, the pleasure spurted through her in joyous waves.

After a while, he shifted them both so that he ended up with his legs stretched out as far as they would go in the confines of the tub, his knees bent a bit, and Rosalind straddling his hips. She lowered herself carefully onto his jutting lance and impaled herself upon it. She let herself down gradually, burying him deep inside herself, but taking it slowly to accommodate herself to the size of him and careful of the soreness remaining from the previous effort. But once he was in all the way, she found it less uncomfortable. When she rocked, the water sloshed around them. Lord Jeoffrey sucked in a deep breath and his face tightened with the pleasure of it. She found she loved watching his reaction and cautiously began to move up and down over him. She studied his face, trying to ascertain what seemed to please him the most.

He lifted her just enough to let him slip two fingers between them, into her slit, just above where his cock bridged their bodies. She moaned when they caressed her most sensitive place and made her tension build with his.

They rocked together. She tried to match her movements to the rhythm of his body's reaction until they bounced so hard the water slopped over the sides onto the floor. The coiled need within her built as their speed increased until she felt it break open. She clutched at him, gasping as the waves of climax rolled through her. A moment later, he loosed a roar of satisfaction as he rammed his seed home in her.

Then he collapsed back against the side of the tub and pulled her down and forward until her head rested against his shoulder, her face turned toward him so her lips nuzzled against his neck.

"My lord," she sighed. "You are a very potent man."

She felt the rumble in his chest as he laughed gently. "Thank you for that, lady, but slight not your own efforts in rousing me to such display."

"It took little enough."

"But only because your talent for it is so great."

"Is it, in truth, my lord? I have no practice with such things."

"Then I shiver to think what you shall accomplish when you have had time to work your talent."

He fell silent suddenly and his arms tightened around her. Rosalind wondered if his own words had reminded him, as they'd done for her, of the reality that he wouldn't be the man to benefit from it.

After a few minutes he roused himself and pushed her gently back. "The water is cooling, and my stomach demands nourishment. Are you not hungry, my lady?"

She stared at him a moment and shivered gently. "Aye, my lord," she said softly, feeling sudden regret for something she didn't understand, possibilities sensed that could never come to being.

He didn't recognize or chose not to hear her sadness. He wrapped a cloth around his middle, helped her from the tub and swaddled her in the robe she'd worn to come to him. Then he pulled a cord to summon a servant. When the man knocked at the door, Lord Jeoffrey consulted him for a few minutes.

When the servant had departed, he handed her another cloth for her hair. He took a comb and began to run it through his wet hair. Rosalind went to him and surprised him by removing the comb from his hand. She sat herself in the one comfortable chair at the side of the room and said, "Bring the stool over here and sit, my lord."

He raised his eyebrows but did as she directed.

"No, facing away from me," she said.

When he was seated, she began to comb out his hair, alternating short strokes that ordered the wild strands and separated out tangles, with longer, more sensuous passes performed purely for the pleasure of it. The soft strands felt like silk in her hands as she sorted and smoothed it. While she did so, he leaned back, resting his upper arms on her thighs. She fought the urge to kiss his hair and brush it across her face while she worked on it. When finally it was all in order, he stood and took the comb from her.

"Your turn, now, my lady," he said, nodding for her to take his place on the stool. She did so. Her near-waist-length hair was slightly curly and turned into a mass of tangles after being washed. He was surprisingly gentle in pulling out the knots and seemed to take as much pleasure in the process as she'd done in caring for his. He was nearly done when another knock sounded at the door.

When he called, "Enter," two men and a woman came in, bearing platters of food and pitchers. They set it all out on the table at the side of the room, moved two chairs close to it on either side, and then departed after ascertaining nothing else was needed.

Lord Jeoffrey served her slices of several sorts of meats, a selection of vegetables, and a chunk of fresh, white bread before heaping his own trencher high.

While they ate, Jeoffrey regaled her with stories of his childhood and adventures as a young man in the king's service. She returned a few vignettes from her own childhood, the things she could remember now without breaking down as she had so often in the terrible time after the slaughter of her family.

The food was the best she'd had in quite some time and Rosalind ate her fill.

There was more wine, too, and her head grew fuzzy as she consumed it. Unaccustomed as she was to taking so much strong drink, it had a potent effect on her. The candlelight sometimes grew brighter in her eyes and sometimes the room seemed to dance around her. She stared at the man seated across from her and admitted to herself he was by far the most attractive one she'd ever laid eyes on. She wanted him. And not just for now. Though she'd known him only a day, she suspected she'd be a long time forgetting him. Nay, not so. She'd never forget him. For as long as she lived, if this was all she ever had of him, she wouldn't forget it.

"You have an expressive face, my lady," Jeoffrey said, wiping his mouth and hands on a cloth and then dropping it to the table, "and I see sadness creeping in there. It will not do. Whatever tomorrow may bring tonight is not about sadness. It's for us to enjoy."

He reached across the table and tipped her face toward him. "We've yet to eat the bread pudding." He stuck a finger into the small bowl and scooped up a tiny bit, then brought it to her mouth. She opened for him and sucked the sweet off his finger. If anything had ever pleased her senses so much, she couldn't remember it. When he offered a second bit, she took it eagerly, sucking so hard on his finger, it made a small pop when it withdrew from her mouth.

Before he could get another fingerful, she said, "Wait. It's my turn, my lord." She mimicked his action, plunging her index finger into the bowl of pudding to scoop a few drops of it and bringing it to his mouth. The smile that spread across his face as she offered it to him was even sweeter than the pudding. It struck straight into her heart, setting off a little quiet laughter from pure joy.

He opened his mouth and she put her finger into it. His lips closed slowly, caressingly over the tip. The touch sent strange waves of tingling heat all through her skin. His tongue move across her finger, licking off the pudding, scraping delightful quivers on her flesh.

They took turns feeding the pudding to each other until most of it had disappeared, although some slopped onto the table or their robes. Jeoffrey spotted a small drip that had fallen on her skin, sliding down between her breasts. He stood up and came around the table, then knelt beside her and leaned forward until his tongue reached the spot.

Shivers exploded up and down her spine at the touch. The hunger for him rose again, and she buried her fingers in his hair—soft and silky now that it had dried—forcing his face against her. His tongue moved against her, seeking out the soft curve of breast and feasting on each inch it found.

She never did remember how she came to be lying in his bed, but she never forgot how it felt to have him moving over her, filling her, taking her to the heights of rapture yet again, and then the peace afterward, the solid warmth of him against her, the welcome bulk of his body in her arms.

After a while he rolled off her, extinguished the lone remaining candle and drew her into the circle of his arms. She had only an instant or two of consciousness to consider the changes that had overtaken her that day before she fell asleep. Not long enough to consider how they might affect her future.

Chapter Six

She woke sluggishly, opening her eyes after an interval of considering whether to do so or not. The bed wrapped her in warmth and security. But bright light filled the room and there was no denying morning had broken. She rolled over and realized she was alone in the bed.

Not far away, though, a figure stood in front of the room's only window. Straight, tall and gloriously clothed only in the radiance of sunlight spilling in from outside, Lord Jeoffrey stared outward. Lost in some private contemplation, his body was held tautly, his expression stern. Through the mist of sleep still clotting her eyes and the haze of dust particles swarming in the sunbeam, he seemed to her to shimmer with glints of light sparkling off his golden hair and smooth, tawny skin.

For a transcendent moment he was a creature completely beyond her experience, something more than human, more than normal man. An angel, or a saint, transfigured in the presence of God, perhaps, glowing with power and glory and goodness. Bathed in light, he was radiant. The most beautiful sight she'd ever seen. Tears burned her eyes, whether from joy at being granted the privilege of such a vision, or from sorrow that such a creature should be so far beyond her grasp, she could not have said.

Then he turned and saw her. He stepped toward her, out of the light, and was a man again. A slow smile chased away the hardness of his face, softening it into warmth. He leaned down and kissed her slowly, but backed away when a soft tap sounded at the door. Swathing himself in a robe he pulled from a peg on the wall, he went to the door and accepted a tray with a pitcher and cups, and a basket covered with a napkin. The tantalizing aroma of bread fresh from the oven drifted from it. He set it on a table and returned to stand beside the bed.

"A fine morning, my love. No doubt you're sore and stiff from yesterday. Think you you can rise?"

She rolled over and then started to push herself upward. The bedcovers fell away from her. Despite what they'd shared, she reached for the cover and pulled it across her breasts as she sat. He smiled with gentle humor, found the long-ago discarded shift, brought it to her, and turned his back as she struggled her way into it.

She started to stand and groaned. Oddly though, it wasn't her bottom that bothered her most. "I'm sore and stiff, but can move. The discomfort is primarily…between my legs rather than on my backside."

He nodded and offered an arm to escort her to the small table where breakfast awaited. "My punishments are intended to cause pain at the time but no lasting damage. That aside, you were hard-used yesterday, especially for one with no experience. I should express sorrow for it, but I cannot be fully sincere in so saying. Rather do I regret any hurt done to you, beyond the discipline you deserved."

He assisted her into a seat and went to occupy the other one. Before touching the food, he gathered both her hands into his large ones and looked at her across the small table. "My Lady Rosalind, may I say I admire how whole-heartedly you fulfilled your part of our bargain? I truly hope no harm has been done to you, and I vow I'll do all in my power to ensure you a content future."

She moved one of her hands to clasp it on the outside of his. "I'm grateful, my lord." She wanted to say more, to tell him how she admired him in return, but could find no appropriate words for her sentiments.

For a long moment they held one another's eyes. Rosalind found herself trying to read possible futures in the smoky depths of his. Several scenes rolled through her mind, though only one could she feel ready to welcome with any joy.

At last he nodded. "We'll speak more of the future later. For now, there's cider and bread and cook's plum jam to spread on it."

To divert her attention, he asked about her family and the events of her childhood while they drank cool, sweet cider, and the warm bread. She told him about her brother and sister, mother and father, trying to focus on her early days and not recall that, save her sister, wed to a baron who dwelt far to the north, all were now dead. There were sufficient pleasant times to blunt the pain of the more recent memories. The love and affection her parents had given her would stay with her always. She told him about the practical jokes she and her brother had been wont to play, and had him laughing loudly and long at the stories about her early attempts at cooking.

"Was that rabbit truly so tough not even the hearth dog could pull meat off it?" he asked.

She shrugged. "I suppose he did eventually, by dint of much persistence, gain a few morsels from it. My father threw what remained to the crows and said it took them more than a week to dispose of what usually took no more than an hour."

He slanted a wry eyebrow at her. "And I recall you offered your services as a cook for me?"

"Credit me with having learned from my experiences," she said, and then in the interests of honesty, added, "I seem to have no instinct or gift for it, however. Maniga, our chief cook, regarded me as a trial she had to bear."

"Why was it necessary that you, a lady, should know how to cook? Surely they did not foresee you having to do for yourself?"

"Nay. It was only to provide a better understanding of what was needful for running the household."

"Ah," he said, as though that were a great discovery for him. "Are you finished?" he asked then, seeing she'd consumed all but a few crumbs of the bread on her plate. "We have yet some time for ourselves, and I would like to show you around the grounds. It appears the weather will be pleasant."

She nodded, although she wondered if her abused body would tolerate it. He rang for a servant to retrieve the clothes she'd worn the previous morning and help her dress. He provided cloaks for them both, his swung over plain breeches and shirt. The shirt was a soft blue that warmed the gray of his eyes almost to the same shade. They traversed a long corridor, descended a flight of stairs, crossed the echoing expanse of the empty great hall, and followed a couple more twisting passages before he opened a nearly unmarked door to the outside. Movement actually relieved some of her aches rather than adding to them.

This was apparently a side entrance, perhaps an emergency escape route in case of siege, but it led to a walled garden at the side of the manor house.

Late winter had just given way to spring when Sir William de Railles had invaded her family home. Calculating the time she'd spent as William's guest, the weeks when he'd thought he could persuade her to do his bidding, then the time spent in his dungeon, she guessed it would be late spring, mid-May, now.

The breeze was still cool, but the midmorning sun warmed her back through the cloak. Lord Jeoffrey took her arm and led her down a brushed dirt path between two patches of vegetables. The garden was nicely ordered and thriving. The new plants grew strong and healthy, pushing up strong stalks or spreading bunches of leaves.

They strolled quietly along the paths until they reached the far end of the fenced vegetable plot. He guided her to a gate, where he opened it and they walked through into a wilder area. Spring-flowering trees and shrubs bloomed in wild profusion, showering petals on patches of new green plants. Perennials sending up fiery new shoots. Fragrances of apple and plum blossoms wakened memories of her childhood playing in her mother's orchard. Someone had once done a great deal of work on this area, but then left it on its own. Rampant vines crept across the paths in places and bushes nearly blocked a few. Hardier plants overtook more tender shoots, stealing light and nutrients.

"My father planted it for my mother," Jeoffrey said, frowning at the untended tangles. "Before I was born. But she died just two years later, struggling to give birth to me, and he lost interest thereafter. A few years back I had a gardener work on clearing and restoring it, but we have too few people to spare for such frivolous endeavors." He sighed as though it pained him to admit the lack.

He guided her to a quiet corner at the far end, where an arbor was tucked into a border of quince shrubs. A cut stone bench sat within. The vines twining the rungs of the trellis hadn't yet fully leafed out, so the sun crept in and warmed the area. The stone was still cool as they sat side by side on it.

He took her hand and turned her to face him. His smile was both sweet and sad as he looked into her eyes. His kiss was sweeter yet, but shorter than she would have wished.

He kept hold of her hand, but turned to study the neglected wilderness of the garden. His expression grew stern and bleak. "God or fate is a cruel trickster. I wonder what I've done to deserve to be tormented this way?"

Rosalind had no idea what he meant, but his obvious pain touched a chord of sympathy in her heart. She squeezed his hand gently and asked, "In what are you tormented, my lord? Most would say you have been abundantly blessed: you are a free man, lord of your own estate, plus you are a man of stature and vigorous health, strong and handsome, and it seems you have the loyalty of your people."

He gave her a wry grin before he returned to his contemplation of the rampant shrubbery. "Truth, lady. I am a lord and blessed with some of the virtues you recite. But free? Only if I were such a man as to turn his back on his responsibilities. And that, thanks to my father's hard discipline and stern example, I am not."

He turned his face to the sun and let it warm him, closing his eyes as he spoke again. "I struggle to keep this household in order; to provide for all the people in my care; to protect, clothe and feed them all. To sustain their lives, their hopes, their spirits. Yet, too often if feels as though I am trying to hold back the wind with just my bare hands." He sat up, opened his eyes, picked up a leaf from the ground and began to roll it between his fingers.

"The estate is rich but does not provide enough to support all the people in my care. Nor do we have enough fighting men to secure its borders should a strong lord like de Railles decide to come against us. For most of my adult life—since my father died—I have wrestled with ways to protect and support it. And, now, when I believe the means to be within my grasp, fate or the Lord God puts you in my path." He laughed harshly, with no humor.

"My Lady Rosalind, you are the most beautiful and delightful lady it has been my privilege to meet. You are just such a one as I have dreamed of finding since I was old enough to harbor such fancies. I hoped to meet a person like you and knew it to be most unlikely." He stopped and sighed heavily. "Yet here you are. And I cannot have you in the way I truly want."

He turned to her again. "My lady, were my circumstances otherwise, I should ask you to do me the honor of becoming my wife. You are everything I want and desire, but for one cruel and critical necessity."

"I have no dowry to bring to the marriage," she finished for him. "Nor any powerful alliances to secure your domain."

"Just so," he admitted. "But I have an offer for you, though part of me hesitates even to voice it."

Rosalind sighed as she considered what her future might bring. "I am aware my circumstances are much reduced, my lord," she said. "And my expectations must be commensurately curtailed."

His mouth tightened in a harsh frown for a moment, then he shrugged and drew a long breath. "I fear to insult you. Yet I have little choice in this."

"Then tell me and allow me to consider what choices I have." It was hard, harder than she expected to say the words bravely. The expectation of pain was a knife prodding at her stomach and heart. Fear tensed her throat so the words had to be forced out.

He nodded. "I have offered for the second daughter of the Duke of Barnston. The family is considering my suit. From their view I have few advantages, but I believe the Lady Alys favors me and is pressing the match on her father. Her dowry and her father's support would secure the estate."

He squeezed her hand gently. "I would offer you a choice. I'll escort you to a convent where you might peacefully reside, or to any surviving relatives who might offer you shelter. Or I shall seek to arrange a suitable marriage for you, and whilst we search, you may remain here as part of my household."

"I feel no call from God to take the veil," Rosalind said. "And my only relatives are my sister who is married to a border lord in the north and some distant cousins to the east that I barely know. Either would, I suppose, offer shelter, though not happily."

She met his eyes. "Were I to become part of your household, what role could I fill? You indicated all must earn their keep here. What would I do?"

He looked away, staring at the ground. "I have need of someone for…personal service for me."

"Personal service?"

His handsome mouth twisted into a frown. "Someone to keep my chambers organized, my clothes repaired, my wounds patched up, my business matters in order." He paused a second before adding, "And my bed warm."

He slanted her a glance that plainly showed his feelings about making the request. "I know 'tis a shameful thing to ask.

But I have no other role to offer you in my household. And...for a short time I would have the privilege of your company and service."

"Our arrangement would end with your betrothal?"

He crumpled the leaf he still held, squeezing it so sharply his fingers were stained green. "Or yours, can it be arranged first."

"And would the rest of your household accept me?"

"There would likely be difficulties with some. There are those who will see the arrangement as outrageous and immoral. Perhaps they are correct. For myself, I cannot help but believe the Lord God has offered us this possibility as a gift, a memory of something that will assist us through darker times later in our lives."

He looked at the green mush in his hand. "Others will resent you for what you are. That you walk and speak and conduct yourself as the lady you are. Because you take on the role of a servant, some will be hard on you. There are other considerations as well. You shall have to agree to submit to the household rules and discipline. And there will also be my personal discipline. You already have some notion how stern and strict those are."

"So I do," she admitted. "There is no other role for me here?"

"The cook can always use another scullery maid. It would not do for you, but if your conscience demands, I'll accede to it." He shook his head and tossed the remains of the leaf aside. "I fear none of your choices are happy ones. Yet perhaps there is some hope in them. I would ask for your promise of loyalty and obedience to me, until such time as a betrothal is contracted for either one of us, and in return I promise my loyalty, my protection and my best efforts to ensure a comfortable marriage for you."

Rosalind watched the bits of leaf flutter in the wind and felt they represented herself: crushed, torn, broken, path uncertain. Yet she wouldn't give in to despair. Her situation could be far worse. Sir William de Railles might have proceeded to torture to get her to agree to his wishes; he might have forced her until her will broke; or he might have let her languish forever in that cell, and death would have been her only escape had Jeoffrey not rescued her.

She wanted to stay with him, wanted whatever she could have of him. Even if it should cost her future. He was an unlooked-for miracle in her life, and she agreed with his belief there was a purpose in their having met. Though she tried not to think it, a small ray of hope lurked in the back of her mind that circumstances might fall out so they could be together. She dared not let herself recognize the hope, but it was there. Rosalind had generally been able to get what she wanted from a family that loved and indulged her, and though the family was gone, she wanted Lord Jeoffrey Blaisdell more than she'd ever wanted anything in her life.

"I shall be your servant," she said to him.

"I wonder if you truly understand the difficulty of what you undertake in this," he said.

"I doubt I do, my lord," she admitted. "But I have been acknowledged to be quick at learning."

"You may find the challenges greater than you expect."

"Then the rewards should be greater as well."

He frowned at her and shook his head. "Lady, please, indulge not a hope that cannot be. Court not the heartbreak such a longing could bring."

"I shall be content to see what the future holds."

He gathered her hands in his again. "For myself, I shall endeavor to rejoice in what the present holds. You are certain this is your choice, of your own free will?"

"Aye, I am, my lord."

"So be it, then." He turned to her and raised their joined hands between them. "My Lady Rosalind Hamilton, in return for your promise of loyalty and obedience, before God I promise you my best efforts to procure a suitable marriage for you, and I promise you my loyalty and the protection of my household until such time as a betrothal is contracted for one of us. On my soul I do make this promise to you."

She had to fight to get her words through a throat that seemed to have tightened against the passage of air. "Lord Jeoffrey Blaisdell, in return for your promise of loyalty, protection and the security of my future, before God I promise you my service, my loyalty and my obedience until such time as a betrothal is contracted for one of us. On my soul I do make this promise to you."

She stared at their joined hands. Hers were nearly invisible, cradled between his much bigger ones. Her eyes burned and a single tear ran hotly down her cheek. She didn't know if joy or sorrow produced it, only knew she'd never forget this moment as long as she lived.

A warm breeze suddenly wafted around them, lifting their hair and clothes, brushing face and joined hands, bestowing a gentle benediction on their temporary union.

Jeoffrey dropped her hands and reached over to flick away the tear, before he framed her face with his palms. His kiss was gentle, a confirmation of his promise and gratitude for hers.

He drew back after a moment, but they continued to study each other in silence. She knew not what he read in her expression, but in his eyes she saw things she knew he'd never put into words, satisfaction and yearning, hope and fear, determination tempered with a trickle of doubt. Whatever happened in the future, she was determined to repay his kindness with as much assistance, support and efforts to please him as she could manage in the time they had.

After a while, he glanced back up at the house and straightened his shoulders. "My time of freedom is done now, and I have duties to see to. I have a few tasks for you now, and I shall introduce you to the household at dinner this evening. Be warned, though: you will not be considered a true member of the household until we have had a session of justice and you see for yourself what you agree to in joining us."

His expression darkened again when he turned to face her and look into her eyes. "I hope you do not come to hate me before our time ends."

Chapter Seven

Dinner was a jovial affair, with most of the household gathering in the great hall for the meal. Jests and snatches of song and laughter burst out between and during courses of fragrant soup, savory roast fowl, fish, flavorful vegetables and sweet pies. A piper and fiddler played merry tunes at intervals, and a fine ale flowed freely. Before the feast began, Lord Jeoffrey had introduced her to the gathered assembly, then acquainted her individually with his fighting men and advisors, including Sir Philip de Mont Charles, a dark, handsome, stern-faced man, whom he identified as his closest friend.

She was seated at the main table with Jeoffrey and his knights, though positioned on his left side rather than the spot on the right his lawful wedded wife would someday occupy. Sir Philip and the other men at the table kept her occupied with jokes, suggestions for trying bits of this and bites of that, and some light flirtation, but she felt keenly the eyes of the other members of the household upon her. Some stares held only curiosity, a few admiration, but most were dubious or even hostile.

There were no petitions for justice that evening, or the next. Two more days would pass before that event arose. She spent most of the intervening time in the quarters they now shared, repairing Lord Jeoffrey's clothes, fixing tears, restoring seams, darning socks and folding over ragged hems. She tried to converse with the serving girl who appeared at intervals to refill the water pitchers and serve her lunch, but the child was too shy and in awe of her to do more than nod and giggle, so she learned little of the household in that time. Though they shared a bed and he held her in his arms, he did no more than touch and kiss her for the next two days. When she asked him about it, he said he did so to allow her time to heal.

The day after they had made their promises to each other, at Lord Jeoffrey's request, Ferris, the majordomo she'd met her first day, conducted her on a tour of the keep. The building wasn't quite large enough to be a castle, but too big to truly be called just a manor, and insufficiently fortified to be a fortress. It was large enough to be confusing, however, and the head servant helped her sort out how to get to the most important places. It was also plainly decorated, somewhat drafty and ornamented with few of the tapestries and pieces of art which had graced the walls of her father's manor.

Aside from pointing out which corridors went where, and introducing her to the chief cook, head housekeeper, a couple of maids and the chief groom who was in the kitchen for a late breakfast, Ferris volunteered little information. He answered her questions as briefly as possible. Rosalind quickly placed him in the camp of those who disapproved either of her personally or of her relationship with their Lord.

The justice session occurred on the fourth day after her arrival and was held, as he'd told her, after dinner. On the afternoon following her morning tour with Ferris, Jeoffrey informed her he'd received two petitions for redress and would hear them that evening. With such a prospect hanging over it, Rosalind expected the meal to be full of dread or anticipation. In fact, the laughing, joking, and music went on just as usual. Nothing very different occurred until after sweets were consumed and Jeoffrey pounded on his table for attention.

He announced his receipt of the petitions for redress. He took the less serious charge first. One of the cook's assistants had thrown a temper tantrum over another servant's request and had broken several dishes. Lord Jeoffrey listened carefully to the cook's account of events, heard the woman's own story, and allowed others who'd been nearby at the time to give their version of events. He asked a few questions to help clarify what had happened and why. He finally determined the woman had been careless with household items but not willfully malicious, and ordered her to receive five mild lashes with a strap.

When he asked if she had any comment, she bent her head toward him and then toward the cook and apologized for her behavior, promising that it wouldn't happen again.

Two young men brought a bench forward into the open area formed by the U-shaped group of tables. The sinner was assisted to bend over it and her skirts lifted. She wore a peculiar undergarment, a set of tight-fitting drawers with a button-fastened panel over the buttocks. When the two buttons at the top were undone, the panel dropped down to reveal the bulk of the woman's bare bottom-cheeks while the rest of the garment remained in place to preserve her modesty.

The victim made no protest or request for mercy as she grasped the sides of the bench tightly. The head groom stepped forward, holding a leather strap that looked like a belt for an unusually large person. At Jeoffrey's nod, he double the strap over, raised his arm and brought the leather down sharply on the woman's bottom. It cracked as it snapped on her flesh but the woman made no sound. She flinched slightly then was still. The second lash was delivered with the same force, something considerably less, Rosalind guessed, than the full power of the groom's arm. The next three followed at measured intervals, all at the same force. The woman made no sound throughout, but sighed heavily when the groom restored the flap to its closed position and helped her to rise.

She stood for a moment facing Lord Jeoffrey. He smiled at her and said, "Well done. 'Tis over." In a voice that carried and was meant for everyone in the hall, he said, "The incident is closed and will not be mentioned again." He nodded for the woman to go and she turned and walked from the room, a flush on her cheeks, which she tried to hide in her hands.

Rosalind couldn't help staring at Lord Jeoffrey as he stood at the head table waiting for the persons involved in the next case to come forward. His smile had conveyed an extraordinary degree of warmth, concern and forgiveness to the woman. To be the recipient of such an expression, Rosalind would willingly take a much heavier punishment than the light strapping the young woman had just endured.

The second case of the evening would be more serious. A young assistant herdsman had been found off flirting with one of the maids while he was supposed to be guarding the stock. He was fortunate no harm had come to the cattle during his inattention, but the results could have been devastating. The maid was off duty at the time and unaware he was not, so no blame accrued to her.

Once again, Lord Jeoffrey listened to the accuser's story, the accused's, and then sought out as much information from others as possible before rendering his decision. Before voicing it, he called the young man to come forward and stand in front of him. Only those at the head table could hear him ask, "What came over you, Gerard? This isn't like you."

The young man, who was probably no more than twenty, shrugged, but his expression showed more care. "I had...I had just had enough of watching sheep and cows, my lord. I needed a change, but Master Thomas said...It was not possible."

Jeoffrey studied him a moment before nodding. "Come and see me tomorrow morning. Perhaps we can make some adjustments." He drew a long breath and let it out on a sigh. "Next time, pray come and see me before you do something so stupid."

He spoke louder when he announced, "Though you acted like a child, Gerard, you're a man and should be taking a man's approach to your responsibilities. Therefore you must be punished as a man for your failures. Two dozen with the whip would be my assignment for such a dereliction. However, since this is the first time you have disappointed us in this way, I shall let it stand at a dozen."

The young man paled a bit but kept himself standing straight. "I thank you for the mercy, my lord," he murmured.

Jeoffrey nodded. "Strip to the waist and go to the post," he ordered.

The two men who'd brought the bench for the earlier punishment escorted Gerard to the designated post, which turned out to be one of the pillars holding up the great hall's roof. A set of iron rings were set into it. Neither of the two men pushed, pulled or even touched Gerard, allowing him to make a dignified approach to it. They waited on either side of him while the young man shed his shirt, revealing a thin body just developing a man's broad shoulders and deep chest. Only when he'd put his arms up to be attached to the pole, did the two men move in and snap the manacles on his wrists.

Rosalind had occasionally witnessed a flogging ordered by her father for some serious offense. It tended to be an ugly, brutal, bloody business and she hated it. She wanted to shut her eyes as the groom approached, having exchanged the strap of earlier for a long, thin, single-tailed whip that could shred the boy's back. Pity compelled her to watch, however, and she flinched when the groom pulled back his arm, sent the lash sailing and let it snap against flesh. A long, angry-red weal spanned the young man's shoulders, but no blood seeped from it.

Subsequent lashes had the same effect, leaving painful-looking welts but only one broke the skin, a small cut that seeped just a few red drops. She recalled Jeoffrey's words that his punishments were intended to cause pain but no damage. It hadn't occurred to her he would mean that so definitely and literally.

By the time it was over the young man wore a lacing of sore-looking welts that would hurt for a few days but leave no scars. Jeoffrey went to stand beside Gerard as the two men released him and caught the boy when he staggered. None of them heard what he whispered in the young man's ear, but he supported the somewhat dazed victim until he was able to stand on his own. Then he handed him over to one of the two men standing nearby and gave some more quiet instructions. As they left the room, Jeoffrey returned to the head table and looked around.

"This, too, is now over and will not be talked of again. Are there any other matters requiring my attention?"

When no one spoke up, he dipped his head and announced it was done and he planned to retire. He stood up and nodded to Rosalind. While the others dispersed to their quarters or duties, she followed Lord Jeoffrey along the hall and up the stairs to his solar.

Once the door was shut behind them, he gathered her into his arms and held her in a firm, enveloping hug for some time. She was surprised to feel his body shake. He sighed heavily and she shifted against his chest until she felt the pounding of his heart. It settled to a more quiet, easy rhythm over the next few minutes, as he relaxed in her hold and his shaking settled. "That is probably the most difficult part of being the lord of this keep," he said to her. "Fortunately these were easy to settle, but sometimes it's very difficult to find what the truth is and to decide on a fitting punishment."

"I thought you did an excellent job of attempting to determine the truth of the situation in each case and learning of all factors that might influence how it should be dealt with. I was all admiration."

"My thanks, my lady," he said. "But these were easy cases. Not all are so. And I know I have punished innocent parties at times, and allowed others who were guilty to escape unscathed." He hesitated, buried his face in her shoulder and said, "I always fear making an error in judgment and harming someone thereby."

"A lord you may be, but a man you remain as well," she said. "Only God can administer perfect justice, yet men must still endeavor to do so to maintain order. Few lords make such an effort to be fair about it as do you."

He lifted his head to smile at her. The warmth of it and the need she saw in his expression reached into her and touched her heart. "My lady, Rosalind, I have tried to allow you time to heal, but I have need of you tonight. Think you you can tolerate my invasion?"

"My lord, I can do that and more." She reached for the belt holding his overtunic in place, releasing it, pulled it off him, and then tugged loose the laces of his shirt. "Would you give yourself into my care tonight?"

One dark-blond eyebrow rose as he considered. A lopsided smile spread slowly across his face and he nodded.

"First we must rid you of these encumbrances," she said, tugging his shirt over his head. Because he was considerably taller, he bent to let her slide it off more easily. His grin grew and became more amazed as she pushed him onto the bed and removed his boots. He obligingly wriggled his hips to allow her to strip off his breeches. The powerful body thus revealed near robbed her of breath. She reached to run a hand down his chest, but he grabbed her wrist, halting the attempt.

"A condition, Rosalind. You must be in the same state of dress as I. I'll build up the fire to keep you warm."

He was as good as word, and Rosalind had the pleasure of watching muscles play under his skin while he lifted hunks of wood and tossed them on the blaze until it roared up and the warmth poured from it. She required his help in releasing hooks at the back of her clothes, but eventually she, too, shed all encumbrances.

"Now, down again, my lord," she instructed him.

"Jeoffrey," he murmured. "Jeoffrey, when we are alone and private. What say you, Rosalind?"

She blushed lightly at the intimacy of using their names rather than titles in private. "I say you leave me nearly speechless, Jeoffrey."

"Ah, I doubt that." The words ended in a sigh as she reached for him and brushed a hand over his chest, letting her fingers rake through the light furring of blond hair there.

Heat poured over her body, from the fireplace, but also from somewhere deep inside. That place responded to the man, admired his body, wondered at his intelligence, valued his efforts at justice, treasured his humor and craved the care he showed toward her.

She sat on the edge of the platform bed and turned to face him, studying his face and body with unabashed delight. His skin glowed tawny gold in the firelight, accented by the brighter sheen of blond hair. Hard shoulder muscles rippled as she brushed careful hands along them, tracing the fine line of throat and collarbone down to his arm. The hard brown nipples fascinated her. He drew breath sharply and flinched when she circled them with her fingers and tweaked, but he made no move to stop her.

When she ran the tip of a finger along his compressed lips, he stared at her, and the hard line of his mouth relaxed into a smile. The smoky gray of his eyes reflected the firelight in wicked glints. She leaned forward to kiss him, and he put a hand on the back of her head to hold her in place while she probed gently at his mouth, parting his lips with her tongue and exploring the mysteries within. Not content, she moved away from his mouth, trailing kisses down along his bristly cheek to the softer skin of his neck. The pulse in his throat throbbed invitingly under her probing tongue, while his earlobe made a soft, tender contrast.

He dropped his hand to his side when she drew back. She sucked in a breath and let it out on a long sigh of joy and doubt, staring at his pleasure-tensed face, then reached over to lay her palm on his flat stomach. He stilled and waited. It took her a few moments to work up the nerve to move her hand lower, letting her fingers creep across his belly, smoothing the lighter tangle of hair there until they reached the jutting length of his hardened cock.

He flinched and moaned at the touch. She glanced at him to make sure she hadn't done harm, but he gave her a nod. Thus encouraged, she reached for him again and wrapped her fingers around his proudly erect flesh. She thought his cock much like the man himself, smooth, almost soft to look at and feel, but strong beneath and hard when needed. The length and breadth of his rod still amazed her. How could all that sizeable mass fit inside her?

His breath grew ragged when she let her fingers roam up and down, trying the smoothness of the bulbous tip, searching the shaft for the most sensitive areas, investigating the full, heavy sacs below, hair-roughened, yet softly vulnerable. His cock began to throb under her caresses, and she brushed her cupped hand up and down it, speeding up to keep pace with his writhing.

After just a few minutes of that, he suddenly reached up and took her wrist, holding it firmly enough to stay her hand.

"No more, Rosalind. I'm like to burst."

She paused, unsure what to do next. He reached over and tugged her toward him, lifting one of her legs as he rolled her over until she sat astride him, her hollow positioned directly above his rod. The tip of him caressed the sweet spot between her legs just as his hands reached up to cup her breasts, fingers stroking the nipples until they hardened. The pleasurable sensations rippled over her body like running water, pouring through every vein and muscle. She leaned forward to take control of his mouth again.

The sweetness filled her in waves of ecstasy. She clung to him and moved over him, straining for closer union. He helped her raise herself to a near sitting position, ready to receive him, and then she carefully lowered herself onto his shaft. The fit was tight, but she let him in slowly, waiting for the pain she'd had on those first occasions. None came. After a few smooth strokes, he slid into her, embedded himself in her.

He watched her, waiting until he was sure she was comfortable holding him, then he pushed upward gently.

Stabs of pleasure like lightning bolts tore through her; building a tightness and tension that made her shake as hard as he was. She clung to his arms, leaning forward to press the tips of her breasts against his chest, rocking against him. He let her set the pace, but she couldn't restrain herself long and began to ride faster and faster, until they burst together past the barriers of everyday life, into a universe of color and joy beyond holding.

Afterward she tipped forward, resting on his chest, her sweat-slicked body tight against his, while their breathing slowed to a more normal pace. His arms enfolded her in the circle of his heat and protection. The peace and sense of closeness sank into her soul while small aftershocks rolled gently through her.

Later still she moved off him, shifted to his side and let him wrap her in the warmth of the blanket and his arms.

Chapter Eight

In the morning they woke with the first light of the sun. Before they rose they lay for a while, watching each other. Even with hair rumpled, eyes still puffy from sleep, and chin bristling with blond whiskers, he made something inside her convulse with the longing to touch him and draw him into her embrace.

His fingers brushed along her breasts, rousing the hunger for him again, then slid down to her slit. His whiskers rasped against the undersides of her breasts as he tongued the nipples, and the mild burn added to the delightful heat he roused in her.

By the time he slid into her, she throbbed with the need for him. He didn't start gently, but buried himself as deeply as he could in one long, smooth stroke. His cock hit a spot inside her that made her body tighten even more and tremble with need. A few more long strokes, finding that wonderful spot again and again, and she broke into another space where she floated in an exhilarating peace while her body continued to spasm in waves of pleasure.

Jeoffrey roared at nearly the same time, spilling his seed inside her. He collapsed into the circle of her arms and rested his head on her shoulder. She cradled him, brushing her fingers through the tangled, silky strands of his hair.

She could have happily stayed with him that way for the rest of the day, but duty called them both.

When they'd washed, dressed, and broken their fast with bread and cider, he took leave of her, saying he needed to check on some of his tenants. Jeoffrey gave her a list of tasks to do while he was gone, including ascertaining a hot bath would await him on his return that evening.

Once he'd ridden out, Rosalind began sorting through the chest of his clothes to neaten and organize them while checking for items that needed to be repaired or replaced. She found an odd, shivery excitement in the intimacy of invading his most personal belongings. It required a stern lecture to herself about the dangers of indulging impossible dreams to get her back to reality.

The task of sorting through and organizing his clothing took most of the morning. After a midday meal of plain bread, a small bit of cold meat and an apple, delivered to their shared quarters by the same tongue-tied servant as usually came, she worked on repairing the items on the stack she'd made. In mid-afternoon, she ran out of thread, and went in search of more.

She had to ask a housemaid and one of the cook's assistants where to find the head housekeeper before she finally located the woman supervising a group of servants making candles.

Elspeth listened to her request with one ear while keeping her eyes on the vat of tallow and the girl stirring it. The housekeeper turned to look her over when Rosalind finished her request, her mouth pursed into a tight frown, eyes contemptuous. Finally the woman sniffed, called over another housemaid and told her to show Rosalind to the linen supply store.

"Mind you take only what you need for his lordship's repairs and no more," the housekeeper enjoined as they turned to go. "We have naught so much to give anyone who thinks they might have a right to whatever they will."

Rosalind, who'd begun to walk away, turned back to the woman. Elspeth watched her with an unfriendly glare. The words to reprimand the housekeeper for her forwardness rose to Rosalind's tongue, but she checked them. She had no position anymore, she reminded herself. For all the world, she was now no more than any other servant, and the housekeeper had every right to remind her of the reality of her position.

Rosalind sighed and caught up with the girl who'd been sent to guide her.

At least this young woman, probably only a year or two younger than her own nineteen years, was more friendly. "I'm Glennys, my... er ma'am," the girl said, fumbling over how she should address Rosalind. Because there was no malice in her confusion, Rosalind smiled at her and said, "I'm Rosalind. Once it was Lady Rosalind, but that life is behind me now. Call me Rosalind."

"Yes, ma... er, Rosalind. You mustn't mind Elspeth so much. Her disposition isn't the best on the days her joints pain her. She's not bad, really. She tries to be fair at least. My cousin works in Sir William de Railles' kitchens, and the stories I've heard from her! I won't say too much on those, but some would make your skin crawl. 'Tis enough to make me know how lucky I am to be here."

The girl looked at Rosalind, looking to see if a rebuke for her forwardness or chatter was coming. When it didn't, she continued. "All do try to be fair here or they do not last long. Sir Jeoffrey insists on it. I know I am fortunate to be in his household. And isn't he a handsome one? So big and strong... And those eyes, they—" She stopped abruptly and blushed. "Of course, you're with him so much more, I'm sure you know."

Rosalind took pity on the girl's embarrassment. "He is a handsome man; perhaps the most handsome I have ever seen. But more importantly, he is a good man, one who tries to be fair and just and do the right thing to protect his people. You may not know, but those are qualities too rarely found in lords of manors. Most are interested only in what suits them best or advances their own ambitions or cravings."

Glennys nodded agreement. "I haven't been out much in the world, mum, but I've heard stories. Some would curl your toes to hear. I know what you say is true, despite what the priests and the church try to teach us."

The girl suddenly paused before a closed door. She knocked softly and pushed the handle down. Five women looked up from various projects as they entered. One woman spun wool into thread, two operated weaving looms and two others were sewing pieces of cloth together. All stared at Rosalind as she and Glennys entered the room, but none offered a smile or a greeting. Knowing how gossip spread through a household, Rosalind was sure they were aware of who she was.

"Ladies," she said, offering them that courtesy. Only one even nodded in return. The others just stared. Rosalind felt their disapproval or resentment of her as a weight on her shoulders, but she just stood straighter and tried not to return their animosity with haughtiness.

"Lady R... Rosalind needs more thread to repair Lord Jeoffrey's garments," Glennys announced. The women made no response but all looked toward the cupboard where apparently such items were stored.

Glennys took the spool Rosalind had brought down and wound onto it thread from one of the large spools in the cupboard until Rosalind nodded that the quantity was sufficient. Glennys broke the thread with her teeth and handed back the smaller spool.

When Rosalind thanked her for the help, Glennys responded, "Come look out for me whenever you need anything, mum. Though my duties be primarily in the kitchen and that's where you're like to find me most of the time, I'll help in any way I can."

Rosalind thanked her again, truly grateful for the amicability of at least one member of the household. When Glennys went to return to the kitchen, after pointing the way back to the great hall, Rosalind decided to take a few minutes rest outside in the fresh air.

She passed through the kitchen garden, heading for the bench she'd shared with Jeoffrey on her second morning at the manor, where they'd discussed their future and made their promises to each other. The deserted corner of the wild garden had a tranquil silence that fed her soul. Although she passed two men working on the vegetable plots, no one seemed to venture into this area.

Her spirit felt bruised by the reactions of the housekeeper and the women in the sewing hall. Before the devastation Sir William had wrought, she'd always been a favorite, with both her family and the household staff. Her father's housekeeper and servants had treasured her, let her help them out at her will, laughed at her clumsy attempts at the various household tasks and congratulated her on successes.

She missed her family so much. Her father was an easy-going man, given to laughter and jests, one who probably allowed both staff and family too much leeway, but he was well-loved by all. Her mother gave her affection less openly, but she would willingly do anything to help anyone who asked.

The memories of their end were still too painful to endure for long, so she turned her thoughts to her possible future instead and wondered what kind of man Jeoffrey might find for her. A good one, she hoped, one as kind and as affable as Jeoffrey himself. Too much to hope he could find a man as handsome and charming, as clever and intelligent, as fair and demanding as Jeoffrey himself. Though she'd known him not quite a week, he set a standard she doubted any other man could match.

Hard to bear the possibility she'd go to some other man and never see him again. Was there any way she could stay here? Perhaps if she refused to wed another... But he would wed a lady who could bring him the advantages he needed to protect his people, and his sense of rightness would insist he not keep around one who might tempt him to dishonor the marriage vows. Jealousy burned in her stomach toward the unknown woman who would have him. Could any other possibly appreciate as well as she did all the excellent traits that combined to make him a man unlike any other? His wit, his intelligence, his sense of justice, his—

A masculine voice interrupted her reverie. "Are you enjoying the view, Lady Rosalind, or just the peace and stillness?"

Startled, she glanced quickly up at the dark, handsome knight standing nearby. "Sir Philip. I didn't expect to see you here. The practice fields are on the other side of the manor."

"I sometimes need a quiet place and time to gather my own thoughts."

"Then forgive me for invading your retreat," she said, starting to rise.

He looked surprised and held out a hand to stop her. "Nay, forgive me, I meant it not that way. In fact, it was naught but pleasure to find you sitting here. You enhance the garden, my lady."

"You're a well-practiced flatterer, Sir Philip. Would you care to sit?" He smiled and sat next to her on the stone bench, putting a small distance between them.

"You out here often?" he asked. "You enjoy the outdoors and the garden?"

She lifted a shoulder in an inelegant shrug. "I spent... I'm not sure how long, but I think it was at least two weeks in Sir William de Railles' dungeon. I find I now want to pass at least some time each day out-of-doors. I appreciate the view of trees and green fields, the smell of flowers, the feel of the breeze on my face more than I ever expected."

"Ah. Perhaps, that's why your thoughts appeared a long way off, my lady," he said.

"Not so far as all that, Sir Philip."

"They did not seem to be entirely happy thoughts. 'Tis a pity to see a face so lovely as yours marred by sadness."

She met the man's dark eyes, surprised by the sympathy she saw there. She'd thought him one who thrived only on excelling at warrior's skills and charming ladies with his flattering tongue. Apparently Sir Philip had depths she hadn't guessed at. Yet, now that she considered it, she shouldn't be surprised. He was Jeoffrey's best friend, after all.

"I... I am not used to being in the... situation I find myself in now," she admitted. "'Tis not so easy as I would have thought.

The staff is not happy about my presence. No one other than yourself and my lord is even friendly. In the eyes of God I am a sinner, and in the eyes of man, a harlot."

"And in your own eyes, my lady?" Sir Philip asked.

"Ah, there is the heart of the matter," she admitted. "In my own eyes I am not sure. I believe I am just a woman doing what she must to survive. But is it truly so, or do I deceive myself? Lord Jeoffrey would present a great temptation to any woman. And I had another choice. I could have retired to a convent and taken the veil."

"Thus depriving the world of the grace of your beauty."

"There is much other beauty for the eyes of man to feast upon. But I do not believe I have any calling from God to the contemplative life and therefore to take the vows of a convent would be another sort of lie. One I could not countenance."

"So you chose the course that seemed to have the least evil about it." Sir Philip took her hand, and she looked up to meet his eyes again.

"I tell myself I did. Then I ask myself if I am just making excuses for doing what I most wanted to do rather than what was right."

"We do have ways of protecting ourselves from unpleasant facts," Sir Philip mused. "Others frequently have a clearer view of our truth. Have you the courage to ask me how I see you?" he asked. "Beyond the beauty of your outer seeming?"

She saw the kindness in his deep blue eyes, but she saw strength and courage and honesty there as well. He would tell her the truth as he saw it, and he warned her she might not like what he said. But avoiding such knowledge would change nothing whereas acquiring it might allow her to alter what was needed. "How do you see me, Sir Philip?" she asked.

A small smile crooked his mouth into an appealing grin. Some woman would be very fortunate to wed this man.

"I see a lady, gently bred and raised. One who has faced a terrible tragedy and severe trials, and come through them with goodness and honor intact. I see a lady whose entire world has been turned upside down, one struggling to adapt to a new reality, a state for which her upbringing could not prepare her. I see a lady who faces trials yet, for she has a pride that will be difficult to subdue. Spoiled and cosseted as a child, she has only recently had to face adverse circumstances, yet she is one who will continue to face those tests with the honor and honesty and dignity that is so much a part of her. She may not always succeed, but she will learn from her failures and grow."

He squeezed her hand a little. "More than anything else, though, I see someone who has made a man I love as a brother happier than he has ever been in his life. For that I owe you much."

"You owe me naught for that," she answered. "My time with my lord has provided its own rewards. I only wish…"

He waited for her to finish the thought, but when she did not, he ventured his own conclusion. "That it could be more lasting?"

"It's selfish of me, I know," she admitted. "I understand why he must have a wife who can bring lands or fortune to him. Yet a part of me yearns to be his in every possible way for always." She drew a deep breath. "I think a part of me always will belong to him."

"In so short a time you've formed so deep an attachment?"

"You know Lord Jeoffrey. Can you not believe it?"

"I know him, but I was not as sure of you." Sir Philip stood. She expected him to go away, but instead he offered her a hand and said, "Walk with me a bit. There are things you should know that Jeoffrey will never tell you. Perhaps when you understand, we can even… But, no, that is not for now."

Rosalind allowed Sir Philip to guide her around the stone paths lining the wildest part of the garden.

"I met Jeoffrey when we both came to Sir Roger Hartman's manor to serve as squires," Sir Philip said. "We were maybe ten, eleven, at the time. When we finally won our titles, my entire family came to see me dubbed. No one came for him. His father sent some excuse; I remember not what it was. Jeoff was not surprised. He had not expected anyone to come. He never expected anything from anyone that I can recall save from himself. Of himself he expected and demanded perfection. He asked for it from others, too, and by the force of his will or personality, he often obtained what he requested, save for what he wanted most from his father."

Sir Philip stopped a moment and they looked out toward a nearby stream. "Jeoffrey grew up here, but it was not an easy thing for him. His father held him responsible for his mother's death and never forgave him for it, never let him forget it. He demanded perfection from him, and was fearfully hard on him when he failed. And what lively, spirited boy does not… test the limits at times?"

"I can imagine you both did your fair share of… testing," Rosalind commented.

Sir Philip just grinned. "Aye, that we did. Yet, except where his son was concerned, Jeoffrey's father was a fair and just man, much as his son is. Jeoffrey learned the lesson well, but he never felt himself worthy to follow where his father had gone. He could never meet his father's expectations of him." The knight became visibly angry on the next words. "No man could have. Yet I have never been able to make Jeoffrey see that."

He sighed. "Jeoffrey almost never speaks of this, mind you. I learned most of it one night when we made our way to a nearby tavern and tested our manhood against the local ale for the first time. The ale, of course, had the last word. We both nursed sore heads and aching bellies the next day. But that night, while deep in our cups, Jeoff finally talked about his childhood and his father's expectations for his only son, and how he could never measure up to them."

"That does help explain some things about him. How long has he been lord here?" Rosalind asked.

"Three years some. We were both twenty-two at the time, becoming bored, and we planned to join with the king's army heading for the continent, but just before we were to leave, Jeoff got word of his father's death. He asked me to come with him here. Sir William had just taken Morton's Hill, his first manor, and we all knew he would not stop there. Jeoff feared there would not be enough fighting men to protect Blaisdell should Sir William set his sights on it. Fortunately, Sir William's sights have been trained mostly on the east, sparing us, so far."

"Not so fortunate for my family."

He groaned a little and dipped his head. "My pardon, lady. I'd forgotten. What was fortunate for us meant devastation for your family."

"'Tis done now and cannot be undone."

"Yet the effects of many deeds linger, as did the old Lord Orland's treatment of his son." A breeze played around them, and Philip reached up to push dark hair out of his eyes. "I believe Jeoffrey is sterner and harder on himself and his people than he needs to be, but that is not my judgment to make. I wish he could be more…"

"Merciful?"

"Nay, he shows mercy enough where 'tis called for. More at ease with himself and others. More able to relax. Less completely bound by duty to everyone else but himself." He turned to face her again. "Which is why I am grateful to you. For the first time I begin to see signs that it could be so."

"Yet, in fact, what he sees as his duty ensures we will not be together long."

A muscle flexed in Philip's cheek as he stared over at the stream again. "Perhaps we might change what he feels duty demands of him."

Rosalind wanted to deny the stirring of hope the words roused, but found she couldn't. "Think you there is a way?"

"Perhaps. Jeoff has it in him to be a great leader. Alliances need not be made solely from marriage. If he were willing to do so, he might find other sorts could serve him just as well."

"I know not that I understand you," Rosalind admitted.

His grin was modest, self-deprecating and a bit wry. "Perhaps I do not understand completely myself. The thought needs more development. But I believe the right path is along that way."

"May I say I hope very much you are right?" Rosalind turned to look to the west where the sun rode low over the treetops. "But now I believe duty calls me back inside. My lord will return soon and he enjoined me have a bath prepared for him."

Sir Philip nodded but caught her hand again. "By all means go and make sure there is a gracious plenty of hot water prepared. He is almighty partial to soaking in water that would singe the skin from your toes." He lifted her hand to his lips and kissed the back gently. "My lady, if you need anything, even just a sympathetic ear, please feel free to call on me."

Rosalind had just time enough to get the bath organized before the servant came to tell her the master approached and would be within the gates in minutes. By the time he entered their quarters, the bath awaited him with ample hot water, fragrant soap and a Turkish towel at the ready.

Jeoffrey's clothes were rumpled and mud-spattered. His hair had come loose from the leather thong and strands waved limply around his face. His shoulders and eyelids both sagged. He looked so tired he could barely hold himself upright. She led him to the chair across the room, pushed him down onto it, kissed him, and then went to drag his boots off. He didn't say anything as she continued with his tunic and shirt, stripping him layer by layer, but he watched her the entire time and cooperated when she asked him to move this way or that. Finally she had him stand and she dragged off his breeches before she led him to the tub. She poured in the last few buckets of water to make sure it was hot enough for him, and then helped him climb in.

He settled into it with a long, deep sigh. "Would you ring for someone to bring me a bit of bread and cheese?" he asked. "I've had little to eat since I set out this morning."

"Did no one feed you on your visits?"

"Several offered." He slid further down into the water until only his head was above it. "But I could tell all were low on provisions, so I ate no more than a morsel or two at each place."

Rosalind answered the knock on the door that followed soon after and conveyed Lord Jeoffrey's wishes to the housemaid. She dragged a stool over to the side of the tub. Sitting on it, she could comfortably reach him with the scrubbing rag she picked up. Trying not to disturb him, she began to wash the stresses of the day off his body.

Strange, she mused, how satisfying it was to care for him in this way. While running the soap-doused cloth over his chest and arms, she indulged a surprising possessiveness about the man. It might not always be so, but at that moment, he was wholly hers, and she treasured him. Treasured every last inch of him. Even the rather large feet and nicely formed toes, the sharp elbows, rough knees, and big ears. Fortunately he kept his eyes closed while she washed him, so he didn't see the emotion that must have been plain to read on her face.

She lavished special attention on his feet, washing them with care, working the cloth in and out around his toes. She concentrated on the job so closely she didn't noticed when he opened his eyes. A few minutes later she looked up and found him studying her. His expression told her more clearly than words how much he appreciated her care for him.

He moved to sit up straighter and reach for her.

"Nay, my lord," she ordered, putting a firm hand on his chest to push him back down. "Rest."

She ran the cloth up his legs, moving around to the side of the tub once she got beyond his knees. He sucked in a sharp, hard breath as the wash rag traveled up his thigh. Staring down through the water, she could clearly see his cock enlarging. He groaned when she washed around his balls, caressing them gently, and began to pant as she scrubbed carefully along the swollen flesh of his shaft.

He seemed to enjoy the rasp of the cloth along his cock. It began to throb in her hand. She wrapped her fingers around him and pumped up and down, getting harder and faster, keeping time with the beat of his pulse in the hard length. She felt the pressure mounting, his body growing tenser. He muttered and groaned as his breath came in short gasps. Then he gave a short yell and his seed spurted out into the water.

For a moment he just watched her, his form still tight and tense. Then he settled bonelessly back against the side of the tub, face washed clean of the dirt and stresses of the day. He looked relaxed, peaceful, happy. She moved around to his head and began to wet his hair, running her fingers through the strands.

A knock at the door signaled the arrival of the food, along with the jug of wine she'd added to the order. Rosalind went to the door, brought the tray to the tub, and while he rested, she fed him bits of cheese and bread. She poured a cup of wine for him. He drank while she washed his hair, gently rubbing the soap into it, massaging his scalp and rinsing it afterward, careful that none of the sudsy water ran into his eyes.

By the time he was ready to emerge and dress, life had returned to his features and vigor to his limbs. With just the towel swaddling his middle, he dragged her up against his hard body and kissed her so thoroughly her head reeled with delight. Finally he let her go again with a hard, gusty sigh and began to dress.

"I would do more now, but should I start, I would not want to quit and we are expected for dinner shortly. You've yet to dress for it. And your hair needs some putting back in order. I have something I must see to now, but I shall have your company at table and in bed tonight." His expression promised good things to come.

He started to leave, but then, as though drawn irresistibly, he returned and kissed her yet again, though briefly this time.

Dinner took far too long. Though she normally delighted in the evening entertainments, Rosalind wondered if the food, the stories, the laughter, and the music would ever end.

When finally the meal concluded, she hurried back to their quarters. The fire burned high in the grate, warming the room. The tub had been emptied, but the buckets sitting near the fire were full again and the water was warm. Did Jeoffrey plan to take another bath?

He was another few minutes, but when he entered the room and his eyes met hers, a wicked grin broke across his face. He kissed her, long and hard, then broke away and went to the fire, where he began to dump the buckets of water in the tub.

"Mean you to take another bath, my lord?" she asked.

"Jeoffrey," he reminded her. "Nay, I mean to bathe another, Rosalind. I shall have revenge for the liberties taken with my body earlier."

She took a moment to puzzle it out, but by the time she understood, he'd already come to her side and begun to undo the tapes fastening her houppeland over the shift. He slid the gown off her shoulders, letting it drop onto the floor. She watched his eyes as he undressed her, bewitched by the glints of humor and love lurking in their depths. Once he'd helped her out of her shoes and removed the last of her clothing, he slid an arm below her shoulders, another under her knees, and lifted her off the floor.

He carried her to the tub and lowered her gently into it. After giving her a moment to adjust to the water and relax into it, he brought a cake of perfumed soap and a wash cloth to the tub. He washed her hair first, carefully leaning her head back to wet the strands, working soap through them and massaging it onto her hair. It felt wonderful to have his fingers scrubbing through the strands and kneading her scalp.

Then he began to wash her body, just as she'd done for him earlier, starting with her hands, moving up her arms and lingering for a while on her breasts. The rasp of the cloth across her nipples sent streaks of fire through her body.

He leaned down to press his mouth to hers and his tongue began to explore her lips. She moaned and wriggled when he invaded her mouth and brushed over the insides, touching his tongue to hers. When she was gasping and trying to pull him to her, he backed away and returned to washing her.

He moved around to her feet and began bathing them. After scrubbing each one individually with the cloth, he lifted her foot and gently kissed each toe, drawing it into his mouth and sucking. The heat and suction were delightful, but then he brushed his tongue around one and it went through her like a bolt of lightning. She'd never guessed that part of her body could be so sensitive.

"Your revenge is cruel, Jeoffrey," she gasped. "Remind me to stay in your bad graces."

"Be assured of it," he said, once he'd released her feet, letting them sink down into the water again. His smile held a wild mix of humor and mischief. He washed the rest of her legs, moving slowly along her calves, over her knees and up her thighs. Each brush of the cloth sent more shivers of pleasure tearing through her, making her body become tense with longing for him. Her thighs were a most sensitive area, and his attentions to them a sweet, fiery torture.

Just when she thought she could bear it no longer, he reached into the slit between her legs and found the sensitive bud there. She squealed aloud as his clever fingers brushed back and forth over it, surrounded it and squeezed gently. Her skin confined her too tightly, drawing her into an arc of tension. He rubbed harder, driving her deeper into the chaos of need, until she suddenly exploded with a scream of delight. Waves of pleasure rolled over her, one after the other. She throbbed with it, clenching and releasing spasmodically.

When she finally relaxed and her breathing returned to something close to normal, she opened her eyes to see him watching her. The joy and satisfaction on his face made something clench in her chest. Love for him flooded her being, overwhelming all else. Whether or not they had a future together—and she would do all in her power to try to ensure it—even more important to her was that Jeoffrey should have what would make him happy.

He lifted her from the tub and wrapped her in a warm, soft cloth, patting it gently against her to absorb the remaining water. Her legs wobbled and she could barely stand, but he steadied her as he led her to the bed. She sat on its side. Jeoffrey brought another cloth and toweled her hair until all the excess water was gone from it and the strands began to curl gently.

Then he pulled the damp cloths from her body and left her sitting nude on the bed. She reached for her nightshift, but he stopped her with a hand on her arm.

"Nay, I'm not finished yet."

She watched him go to his garderobe and reach for something at the bottom of it. He pulled out a small glass jar with a cloth stopper. When he removed the cloth, the heady aroma of an exotic perfume drifted from it.

"What is it?" she asked, basking in the lovely fragrance.

"Oil of sandalwood. I bought it from a trader some months ago but had forgotten it until recently. He said he brought it from Persia." He put his finger over the top and upended the jar for a moment. He came to her side and ran the oil-coated finger along her throat and down between her breasts. The aroma hit her even more strongly, dazzling her sense of smell. The smooth glide of it on her flesh roused fresh tingles of anticipation.

He eased her back until she lay sprawled on the bed, then he began anointing her all over with the oil. His fingers slid over her flesh in an uncommonly easy, gentle glide. He circled her breasts, spiraling in toward the center until she tightened to near unbearable tension in anticipation of his reaching the tips. And when his slick fingers did finally brush across them, she moaned in delight as pleasure again struck into her.

By the time he'd gone up and down her legs, into her slit and out again, she could hardly bear it. Just when she was sure another stroke would make her explode he stopped and kissed her. Without his asking she knew what he wanted.

She sat up and pushed him back onto the bed beside her. The oil felt sensuously slick and heavy against her finger when she tipped some out. It let her fingers glide against his skin in a way they never could otherwise, bringing a whole new dimension of pleasure in touching him. The aroma ravished her senses and lifted the experience into something sublimely removed from everyday life.

She made spirals on his chest muscles, working in toward his nipples just as he'd done with her.

He groaned when her oil-smeared palm glided up the length of his cock and then down again. Its heavy length throbbed wildly in her hand.

He couldn't bear it for long and soon pushed her back down and positioned himself over her. With the oil easing its way, his cock slid into her easily and more freely than normal. He took his time with the strokes, moving in and out on a slow rhythm that let pleasure and tension build farther than she thought she could bear.

Finally they yelled at the same time. He spilled his seed into her just as the stars burst once again in her brain and pleasure drowned her in wracking sensation.

Chapter Nine

The next morning he requested her assistance with some business matters needing attention. She followed him down to his office after they washed, dressed, and ate. On learning she had a clear, steady hand, Jeoffrey dictated several messages to her for sending to some of the surrounding manors and estates.

Once that was completed, he asked her to meet with the housekeeper, the butler, and cook to take inventory of their stocks of various supplies. He wanted to know if they had a supply of certain staples sufficient to let them spare some for crofters he'd visited the previous day.

Anticipating that Elspeth wouldn't be happy to see her or eager to cooperate, Rosalind almost protested. But a second thought suggested she needed to learn to deal with his household and the difficult situations it might present. It would be a challenge; one she would face with as much dignity and humility as she could simultaneously muster.

It took some searching, but she finally found the housekeeper in a small storage room in a little-used section of the manor, showing a team of young servants how to clean and wax furniture. One older girl looked on while the youngsters listened. She moved to show one of the smallest girls how to wipe with the grain. Elspeth looked up, saw Rosalind at the door, and nodded at her, but continued the lecture on proper procedures for a few minutes more, until she satisfied herself the youngsters could do the job properly. Then she came to the door where Rosalind waited.

"Beg pardon for keeping you waiting, my lady," she said. "But they are new to the task and will ruin every bit of furniture without proper instruction and guidance." She didn't actually sound especially contrite.

"Of course," Rosalind agreed. "'Tis right they learn the correct method from the start."

The woman's glance was suspicious. "What want you from me, my lady?" she asked.

Rosalind explained the mission Lord Jeoffrey had assigned her, and then added, "And, please. I'm not the lady of this manor. I'm just Rosalind."

The housekeeper sniffed. "A lady you were born, a lady you remain, though you choose to disregard the proper behavior of a lady."

Again Rosalind nearly let loose the rebuke that rose to her tongue but stopped it before the words could do their damage. Arguing the point could serve no purpose, so she simply said, "As you will. Can you get the cook and let us take stock?"

Elspeth nodded. Together they sought out Brenna, the head cook, and Ranulf, an ancient, wizened, deaf and nearly blind little man who bore the title of butler more as a courtesy than for any service he could still provide. They all followed Elspeth to a large storage vault where barrels of flours, meals, dried fruits and vegetables stood in rows like fat soldiers awaiting the call to battle. Vats of ale, beer and wine fermented in an adjoining room.

One by one they glanced into each barrel, noting the contents and the level. Rosalind marked off each on a sheet of paper. Once they'd finished the survey, they sat down and calculated how long until replacement supplies of each could be expected and how many people had to be fed from the remainder until that time. By mid-day, Rosalind had a fair notion of what and how much could be spared.

She thanked Elspeth, Brenna and Ranulf for their assistance. Elspeth grunted a flat, curiously neutral reply, though Rosalind thought—or at least hoped—she saw the beginnings of a certain level of respect for her competence.

Brenna nodded sharply and headed back to the kitchens, while Ranulf gave her a sly wink before toddling on his way. Rosalind returned to Lord Jeoffrey's office and handed him a sheet of paper listing what could be spared for the needy of the estate.

In the afternoon, he had more correspondence waiting for her assistance, although this batch pertained more to the business of running the manor rather than to his political and social associations.

Before they started on the work, though, he stole a few minutes while they were private to kiss her so thoroughly she began to feel balance and awareness slip away. He steadied her and held her until her breath and heartbeat returned to normal.

"I fear duty calls us to less enjoyable pursuits," he said at last. She nodded, drawing a deep breath, and agreed.

"I have some trade agreements to be transcribed." He gave her a list of them, grain to one, eggs to another, and the purchase of several blocks of salt, a few pigs and three horses with another.

"We have a new vat of ale to be disbursed as well," he told her. "The tavern keeper will buy it at a credit of twenty sacks of milled wheat flour. Our ale is greatly prized for superior quality and taste. Its reputation extends throughout the region. I have heard there are some who make the trip here just to taste it." She heard the pride in his voice.

She pulled out one of the confirmations she'd already written and studied it. "Why then do you barter so much of it against just twenty sacks of milled wheat flour?" she asked.

"The miller accepted it as an equal trade," he said. "What of it?"

Rosalind remembered her thrifty mother's strictures about the relative worth of certain items and being careful to ascertain the equivalency of goods being bartered. Equal quantities of most items weren't of equal worth and that valuation often depended on how much others would be willing to pay for the same thing.

"Did Ranulf make this agreement?"

Jeoffrey grimaced. "Ranulf has not been… capable of negotiations of that sort for quit a while. The miller told me this has always been our agreement."

"It appears… somewhat disproportionate. I think perhaps you do not prize your own ale as highly as some of your neighbors do," she suggested. "Have you ascertained what the tavern asks for a pint of it?"

He threw a confused look her way. "Nay. I have worries enough encompassing my own affairs; I have no time to spare for others'."

"Would you object should I ask a few questions of your staff about some of these?" she asked.

"Nay. If you find our ale to be of greater worth than we now ask, I shall accept the increase gladly."

A knock sounded on the door at that moment. Within seconds Ferris escorted a flushed and sweating young stranger into the room. The boy moved to the middle of the open space and bowed. "Lord Jeoffrey. I have a message for you." He held out a rolled piece of paper.

"Bring it here," Jeoffrey said.

He took it from the boy, and said, "My thanks." He signaled to Ferris. "Take care of our friend, here," he said.

The boy grinned in satisfaction as he followed the majordomo from the room.

Rosalind waited while Jeoffrey read the message, which was apparently long and rather complicated. After a lengthy silence, Jeoffrey sat it on his desk and clasped his hands under his chin. His eyes closed for a minute while he thought. He opened them and rang the bell to summon a servant.

Ferris showed up again within moments. "My lord?" he asked.

"Find Sir Philip and ask him to come here," Jeoffrey instructed the man. "Tell him I need him immediately."

"My lord." Ferris bowed and left.

"What is it?" Rosalind asked when she heard him sigh as he opened his eyes to read the message again.

"I'll spare you most of Edward Renfill's bombasity, but the matter of it is thus: Sir William de Railles has annexed the lands east of the Anneth River that belonged to Marwick. It's doubtful Marwick will try to wrest control back since his forces are significantly outmanned by de Railles's. Edward suspects Sir William will next set his sights on Connington since it adjoins the piece of Marwick Sir William now claims."

"And does not Connington adjoin your estate on the west?"

Jeoffrey drew a long breath. "A small corner of it does. Shelton lies between us for most of its length. But Sir William's breath begins to fall on us all."

Sir Philip entered then. He appeared to have been in the midst of a vigorous training session. His dark hair was askew and his shirt unlaced. He wiped sweat off his face, leaving a worried expression behind. "What news?" he asked. "What is wrong?"

Jeoffrey related the gist of the note as he'd done for her. Rosalind watched the expression on Philip's handsome face go from worry to anger and determination.

"His eye turns this way," Philip said. "If he does not yet see us in his plan, it will not be long ere he does."

"Our time is shorter than we had hoped," Jeoffrey said.

Philip watched him, started to say something, stopped and waited a moment, considering the words, then started again. "'Tis time to gather who we can."

"My suit has not yet been answered by the duke."

"Bring him to us anyway," Philip said. "It may be more remote, but ultimately his demesne is threatened by Sir William's ambitions as well." Philip paced from one side of the room to the other as he spoke. He stopped for a moment when he reached one wall, flicked a glance at Rosalind, then watched

Jeoffrey with a keen eye. "We dare not lay all our hopes that way. Especially not now."

Jeoffrey's expression hardened and a flicker of anger crossed his face. "I am not the one—"

Philip cut across his protest. "That need not be decided right now. Our first task is simply to bring all together to decide on a course of action."

"It may not be wise."

"Perhaps not, but no one else has yet taken the straw," Philip stated. "How long can we afford to wait for them? The others are too old or weak or self-absorbed. But if someone younger and more vigorous calls them to consider action that might save them from destruction, they will come."

"What sort of action are you proposing, Sir Philip?" Rosalind asked.

"At the moment, merely a convening of all whose lands and livelihood are threatened by Sir William's ambition. In my own mind, the course we must take is clear, but others do not share my clarity on that." He flicked a significant glance toward Jeoffrey.

"'Tis not the need for action I dispute," Jeoffrey said, "Nor the need for a joining of all our forces. And I chafe to be party to it." He looked down at the note on his desk.

Rosalind frowned at him. "Then why, my lord, do you hesitate over convening such a force?"

Jeoffrey looked at Philip before turning his glance back to her. "There are political complications. I am not... If I take the first action, they will enlist me to lead this combined army."

"I do not understand why that should be such a concern."

Again Philip and Jeoffrey exchanged a glance. "My lord has his reasons," Philip said to Rosalind. "I do not necessarily agree they are *good* reasons, but he has reasons."

"And I did not say I would not do what was needed," Jeoffrey added. "I am not as sure as you what that might be.

Allow that I have more complicated responsibilities." He shot Philip a hard look for a moment. "Not all can afford to turn a blind eye to the political complications of assuming power." He stared at the message on his desk. "But I agree we need to bring all together. The rest is to be decided later."

She had a sudden vision of him in battle, strong and fierce, but still a man and thus vulnerable. A mental picture of him lying on the ground, bleeding from a sword-thrust, set her heartbeat pounding painfully at her chest. It couldn't be and she dared not even think it. She replaced the vision with one of him charging into Sir William's keep, claiming victory over the monster. That view she'd keep firmly in her mind.

"We must band together if we are to have any chance of resisting him," Jeoffrey said, slowly, as though he felt his way through the idea cautiously. "If we who are threatened can go against him as one, we will have the best odds of victory. Rosalind, we have work to do. Invitations must go out immediately. We shall invite all the surrounding lords to meet with us here a fortnight hence to discuss an alliance to resist Sir William."

Sir Philip nodded his satisfaction. "I shall set our men to more vigorous training and let them understand they may soon be tested in earnest."

"Aye," Jeoffrey said. He watched Philip leave, his expression troubled.

Rosalind suspected there was more the two men would have said to each other had she not been there.

Under Jeoffrey's direction, Rosalind spend the rest of the afternoon preparing the invitations. There were quite a number of them. She wrote until her hand and arm hurt, stopping only when the dinner gong sounded. She looked up in surprise that so much time had passed. Jeoffrey also emerged from his absorption in writing some lengthy treatise and laid down his quill.

"I apologize for keeping you so long, Rosalind" he said, coming over to where she sat, rubbing the aching muscles of her shoulder. "And for working you so hard."

"You appeared to be just as engaged, my lord. Think naught of it."

He smiled and leaned over to kiss the back of her neck. "Are you as hungry as I am?"

"I feel I could dispose of an entire haunch of beef on my own." She drew a sharp breath as his tongue swirled against her skin. "But my lord, I fear you mean to distract me, and there is no telling what might happen should you rouse an additional hunger."

He laughed and straightened. "Some things a man dare not risk. Let us proceed to dinner."

She stood. "These are near done. An hour's work should see them all ready to be sent." She did not tell him that she planned to remove a couple of the trade agreements before the messages were sent. She wanted to keep those for a day or two to investigate their equity. None involved supplies at critical levels, so a day or even two would create no crisis.

Chapter Ten

After dinner that evening, Lord Jeoffrey announced the plans for the council. It set off a near-thunderous murmur of astonishment, speculation and plans. Everyone knew there'd be much to be done in a short span of time.

For the next several days, the keep stayed in an uproar of servants scurrying to and fro, exclaiming when needed items weren't available or couldn't be found, arguing over who should be doing what and when, scolding and cajoling the extra staff acquired for the nonce. All the guest rooms had to be aired and prepared for the influx of visitors soon to deluge them. Linens were washed, straw replaced, fireplaces cleaned, flues checked, extra wood laid in. Two young housemaids swept out the great hall and replaced all the straw, cleaned and polished the tables as well as the extra trestles and benches brought in to accommodate the crowd. In fact, nearly everything in the keep was cleaned or polished to a high gloss.

The kitchen staff began a round of baking and cooking that kept interesting aromas circulating through the building. Scullery maids tripped over each as they flew back and forth at the directions of the cook or head baker. Both brick ovens steamed from sun-up to sun-down with loaves of bread, cakes and pies, one replacing another as soon as the previous was done. Several young men and boys stayed busy hauling in and splitting wood to keep the fires burning or stacking it against the coming influx.

All but the absolute essentials were cleared from the courtyards, training fields and gardens to make room for the tents and pavilions that would house some of the guests.

At Jeoffrey's request, Rosalind quietly supervised the activity, but she did it with care to ensure she didn't interfere with or undermine the authority of the upper staff. She consulted with Ranulf and Brenna over supplies that would be needed and how best to procure them, and then sent messengers with offers and orders.

Elspeth had control of the cleaning and preparation of the keep, which proceeded in an organized and efficient manner, so Rosalind mostly stayed out of her way, checking at intervals to ascertain which tasks had been done.

Rosalind also kept track of who had received invitations and the responses that came back, noting not only the names, but how many family members would accompany the lord or squire, how many men-at-arms and servants could be expected as well. Whether they would bring their own pavilions or require quarters within the keep, and how many horses would need stabling. She drew a map of the manor, marking off the location of all guest quarters, extra servants' quarters and any spare rooms that might be converted to guest quarters for the occasion. As the acceptances returned, she began to mark off who should be placed where.

At midweek, she set out before dawn with Lord Jeoffrey, heading to town on market day to speak with some of the merchants and acquire additional supplies. She had a list of items suggested by cook, butler, housekeeper and the seamstresses. While Jeoffrey went off to the saddler and blacksmith, a pair of footmen escorted Rosalind to the open air market, where she spent several delightful hours seeking out the wares she wanted, comparing quality and quantity, bargaining for the best price and being sure she found all she needed.

Whispers and giggles followed wherever she went. Rosalind knew what the young girls and the older women said about her to each other as she passed, and for a short time she allowed it to concern her. She couldn't change what was, so she could do naught about the talk save ignore it.

Whatever they thought of her and her position in Lord Jeoffrey's household, all understood she had his coin and permission to purchase for him. Only two declined to speak or do business with her and those she felt she could safely disregard since neither had anything she couldn't acquire elsewhere.

Though she'd had little practice in the art of buying and selling, she'd watched others do so and listened to their hints and advice. Her mother had always recommended one try to be pleasant with and even befriend those you dealt with. So Rosalind took the time to speak to the various merchants, commenting on quality of the wares, or the pleasant nature of the children hanging around, or even the mildness of the weather when no other topic offered itself.

She asked questions about trades made before and trades with other merchants not present, and listened carefully to what she was told, until she had a fair idea of the relative value of most important commodities. In particular she asked several people their opinion of the Blaisdell ale and the rates the tavern charged for it. At other intervals she asked about milled grain and what that went for. She came away more convinced than before that the agreement with the miller needed to be revised.

By midafternoon she'd acquired or arranged for delivery of everything on her list save the fabric requested by the housekeeper to replace some of the linens too worn to be used. Given the short time until guests arrived, the household weavers—already working to supply necessary items, particularly servants' uniforms which had been allowed to grow a little shabby—couldn't be expected to replace such a quantity of household linens as well, so they'd have to be purchased.

Rosalind had noted the location of several cloth-merchants and she went round to them, discussing fabrics available, quality and price until she found what she wanted at a reasonable cost.

Once the deal for the linen broadcloth was concluded, she asked the merchant about his finer fabrics, and in particular if he had any dyed silks. Due to her thrift and her rapidly improving bargaining skills, she still had a few coins left with everything on her list covered, which meant she could indulge in a thought she'd had earlier. The man nodded and invited her into a small tent behind his stall. She left a footman to wait with the linen while she followed the cloth-merchant into the dim, crowded little space. He moved standing bolts and rolls of fabric aside until he found what he wanted.

"This, Madame?" he asked, holding forth a roll of delicate, sky-blue silk. The color was lovely and the cloth had a fine weave with an excellent sheen, but it wouldn't suit at all.

"The quality is right but not the color," she told him. "Have you anything in a deeper shade?"

He thought for a moment, then sorted through the rolls again. This time he emerged with a smaller bolt of indigo-dyed silk.

She fought down her excitement as she fingered the edge. It was perfect, exactly what she wanted, but it wouldn't do to let the man know that.

"Is this all you have of it?" she asked. "The bolt is a bit small. I know not if the quantity would be adequate. And have you anything darker yet?"

"Alas, Madame, this is as deep as anything I have."

She expected it would be so, but pretended disappointment. "It might do, but I'm not sure. How much do you want for it?"

Although the starting level wasn't as high as she'd expected, she flinched when she heard the price and shook her head sadly. "I don't have that much, sir," she said and made a counter-offer. As anticipated, he looked horrified. He decreased the asking price, however, and lowered it a bit more than she'd hoped. She steeled herself to keep her expression neutral as they reached an agreement that would leave her with just a few small coins remaining.

Because she wanted it to be a surprise, she had the footman roll the bolt of silk inside the broadcloth to hide it. One last stop saw her turn over the last of the coins for a bit of exquisite lace that would set off the silk perfectly.

Just in time, she carefully stored the lace in the cloth bag she carried. When she looked up, she saw Jeoffrey approaching. Though he wore his customary plain clothes, no one mistook him for anything but a lord. People moved out of his way, bowing or curtsying to him, as he crossed the road to meet her.

He eyed the footmen flanking her, noting the loads they bore, then he smiled at her. Her heart did a funny little leap in her chest.

"My lady, I presume from the loads I've seen heaped in the carts and those my men are bearing, your time has been successfully spent?"

"Indeed it has, my lord," she answered.

"Are you done?"

"Aye."

"Good. Let's be on our way, then."

He took her arm and led her toward the place down the road where his carriage waited. The footmen followed behind.

As before, people moved out of their way and paid courtesy to Lord Jeoffrey as they passed. When they looked at her, however, most either stared in contempt or glanced away in quick dismissal.

After the third time it happened, she felt his growing anger in the way the muscles of his arm tightened and the set of his shoulders grew more rigid. His step quickened and his expression darkened into a frown. When another man bowed to him and flicked her a look of amusement mixed with disdain, he moved toward the man, saying, "You, sir, should be—"

Rosalind stepped to Jeoffrey's side and took his arm again. "Please, my lord, let it be. They do nothing wrong, truly."

"They have not the right to judge you that way."

"Perhaps not, but in custom they do only what is usual."

The man he'd approached had wisely removed himself from the way of danger, scuttling out of sight while the lord and lady were occupied with each other. Jeoffrey stood rigid, battling back his anger. Finally after a few tense moments, he drew a deep breath, let it out and relaxed just a shade.

"My apologies, Lady Rosalind," he said. He met her gaze, his gray eyes deep and shadowed. "I did not think adequately on how your position would appear in the eyes of the world, nor how it would affect you."

She tried not to sigh. "Regard it not," she begged. "My position is a great deal improved over the time I spent with Sir William, and for that I am nothing but grateful. My standing in the world may improve in time, but for now, I'm content with things as they are."

He looked at her. "Are you truly, my lady?" he asked, his tone all sincerity. "I know not why you should be. You receive not the respect to which you should be entitled."

"My lord," she said, considering her words carefully, "in the eyes of the world I deserve no more respect than I have been given. But I am in receipt of a love and joy to which, perhaps, I am not entitled but have been given as a gift. That compensates for much."

She looked up at him when he stopped and tensed up again. He looked astonished.

"Love?" he asked.

"Aye. Love. You love me, My Lord Jeoffrey. You would wish it were not so, I know, but 'tis true, nonetheless."

When she tugged on his arm, he began to move again, but he was like a man sleepwalking. "I love you," he said, half-question, half-statement. "And do you love me in return, Lady Rosalind?"

"Aye, that I do."

He made no answer, but suddenly increased the pace of his walk. Rosalind didn't hear what he told the carriage driver, but they quickly outdistanced the carts that had accompanied them, and the return trip was made at a faster pace than the journey the opposite way that morning.

On returning to the manor, Jeoffrey stopped in the kitchen long enough to request a bath, specifying the large tub be brought, before leading her directly to their quarters. They didn't have to wait long before a pair of men brought in a large tub and several more servants followed with buckets of water.

Rosalind and Jeoffrey shared the tub, and a flask of wine, and much merriment. They splashed each other between drinks, giggled, and sang. He taught her several very naughty ditties and they took turns singing them, though in truth neither of them could carry a tune for very long.

As they were getting out, she stepped ahead of him, and wrapped herself in the big towel, leaving him with a much smaller one. She moved to the other side of the room and grinned as he tried to approach her and hold the small towel around his middle at the same time.

"Foul, lady," he cried. "You know that towel is mine. This is barely a handkerchief to cover my privates."

"But it looks so very well on you, my lord."

"That matters naught. You used the wrong towel. I demand you return my towel."

"Perhaps you shall have to come and claim it," she teased.

"If I do so, you will regret you did not concede it to me sooner." His tone conveyed more promise than threat.

"Perhaps," she agreed. "But at least I shall be warm and dry by then."

In mock anger he said, "You shall be warmer yet when I catch you. Your bottom will be especially warmed."

She slid to the side as he got within arms' reach of her, slipping away from him, around the table and chairs, nearing the wardrobe chest. He followed, one hand clutching the tiny towel, grunting and growling, his face screwed into a fierce frown. She couldn't suppress a giggle as the towel slipped and his enlarging member pushed above it.

He finally let the inadequate cover fall to the floor and lunged toward her. Again she eluded him, sliding past the wardrobe and nearing the bed. Avoiding the trap of having the bed at her back or being caught between it and the wall, she angled across the room. A lively chase around the room ensued.

She clutched the towel to her breast as she evaded him time and again, side-stepping or ducking under an outstretched arm to get away.

He caught a handful of the towel and jerked on it to bring her back to him. Instead she let the cloth fall away. For a moment, the sight of her nude body stopped him, then he dropped the towel he'd been so eager to capture and rushed toward her. Again she eluded his grasp and he pursued her around the room twice before he finally grabbed a handful of hair, effectively bringing her to a stop.

Before she could react, he'd let go her hair, wrapped her in a bear hug and lifted her off her feet. He carried her over to the bed, where he sat on the side and stood her on her feet between his legs, facing him.

His breath came in gulps and it took a moment before he could say, "You thought you could escape me, lady? Think it not. Now or ever. But I will have your apology for your impudence in taking what was not yours."

She was even more winded. "Nay… my lord. I have naught to apologize for. Courtesy demands you should offer… me the choice of towels."

"I am lord here! I will have whichever towel I will, and no impudent young lady, however beautiful, will deny me it." The words were hard, but the sparkling lights in his eyes belied any hint of anger or outrage.

"Then perhaps we should be sure there are adequate towels of sufficient size for the two of us," she suggested.

"Perhaps so. And perhaps it will be so next time. For now, though, I still have not heard your apology."

When she attempted to back away, he closed his knees around her and grabbed at her wrists. Moments later she was swept off her feet again, pulled forward and to the side until she ended up draped over his knees, face down, with her feet touching the floor on one side of him and hands on the other.

She let out a small shriek. "What are you doing, my lord?"

"I will have that apology," he reiterated. "If you wish to spare your pretty bottom a warming, you will tender it immediately."

"I told you I see no need for an apology."

"Then perhaps this will help clear your vision."

His hand came down on her bottom in a sharp slap. It wasn't very hard and it stung only a little. She didn't react.

Several more slaps followed quickly, until it was burning just enough to make her wiggle a bit.

"You may halt this at any time by offering that apology," he told her before he rained another series of spanks on her vulnerable posterior.

It was a strange feeling being at his mercy in such a way. It wasn't terribly comfortable. His hard, muscular thighs were no soft pillow, and his erect rod poked her in the belly. Blood rushed to her head and her bottom began to sting. Yet, there was something incredibly exciting about it, too. She could never have imagined the thrill of being at the mercy of a strong, loving man who would take you to the edge of pain but do no harm. And the fire he ignited in her bottom was setting alight other needs and urges as the tingling sensations transmitted themselves throughout her body, settling in her woman's parts between her legs.

Between spanks, he caressed the curves of her bottom with his big, hard hands, sometimes sliding close to the crevice where the source of her pleasure lay.

"Are you prepared to apologize yet?" he asked.

Her "nay" became a squeal as the hand rose and fell harder. He continued to spank her until the burn and the need it roused escalated to a point beyond bearing.

"Halt, please, my lord," she begged at last. "I shall apologize."

He rubbed the stinging flesh that must be bright red from his attentions. "Tender it then."

"My lord, I apologize for taking the cloth meant for your use."

"And you will not do so again?"

"You have your apology. That was all you asked for."

He drew a deep breath and his hand stilled. For a moment he debated, then he muttered a grudging agreement. He reached a hand down to turn and raise her body so she sat on his lap. His arms wrapped around her, drawing her against his chest. He sprinkled soft kisses on the top of her head, working down her brow and temple, across her cheek until he reached her mouth. She leaned out a bit to give him better access.

When his tongue prized open her mouth and invaded that sanctuary, the fire that simmered inside her blazed into furious life.

She wiggled far enough away from him that she could work her hands up his chest to his shoulders where she clutched at him fiercely as the kiss went on and on and her body seemed poised to burst into flame. Need swept over her in a tidal wave of longing.

His hands found her breasts. He stroked, kneaded and pinched delicately until she was writhing in his hold. She let her hands roam back down his body, along chest and belly until she encountered the tip of his cock. It throbbed as she brushed fingers along its long, hard length, rocking up and down, until he, too, was vibrating with need.

He lifted her again and moved her to the bed, then he came down atop her, weight held on his elbows, parted her legs with his knees, and entered her in one long, smooth effort. His breath came in hard gulps as he drew back and plunged into her again and again.

She gasped when the length of him inside her hit a spot that triggered waves of sensation. He paused for a moment and then he wiggled enough to caress her inside. The resulting blast of hot, shocking, vibrating pleasure felt like lightning flashing through her body. It sent her over the edge into a jerking, spasming ecstasy. Two more hard plunges and he joined her, spilling his hot seed within. After a minute he collapsed against her, though he kept his weight on his elbows. His damp chest pressed to hers; his head rested on her shoulder with his hair brushing sweetly at her cheek.

They lay together for a while, joined, but quiet, listening to each other's breathing. She stroked a hand through his hair and let it run down along the smooth, hard muscle of his back. He felt sleek and solid, a welcome pressure all along her body. He turned his head just enough to brush his lips across her cheek. She wished they could stay this way forever.

Rosalind wondered if heaven could hold anything as wonderful as this. She had to presume it did from everything she'd heard from the priests and brothers. Yet she could hardly imagine a wonder and joy to outshine this. She planned to do her best to get there and see.

He drew a deep breath and leaned down to kiss her, brushed hair back off her brow and let his lips wander over her cheek and temple.

A hint of sadness tinged his voice when he spoke. "Aye, I do love you, Lady Rosalind. And how I will be able to let you go when the time comes, I know not."

She hoped he wouldn't be able to. She wasn't proud of herself for harboring that longing. It wasn't a worthy or noble hope. But she could no more eject it from her soul than she could stop her heart from beating.

"Think naught on it for now. Let tomorrow care for its own worries," she advised him.

He relaxed and rolled off her, then pulled her close to him again. "You are wise beyond your years, as well as beautiful," he said.

"Nay," she said on a long sighing breath. "I am not wise. Not wise at all. Just fortunate to have been rescued from hell by a man beyond all my dreams."

She felt rather than saw him nod, since her head was tucked under his chin. "And though in coming years I may have nothing of you but memories, I will still count the day I removed you from Sir William's dungeon as the most fortunate day of my life."

They stayed quiet for a few minutes after that, each lost in quiet longings and dreams. Then he shook her gently.

"Dinner will be waiting on us, and I would not keep the household from their meal." He levered himself up on one arm. "I received a petition for redress to be heard tonight, but the boy in question chose to take himself off rather than face my justice. It's as well."

"What did he do?"

"The master groom asserts he abused one of the horses. A thing I cannot countenance. It would have been a hard lesson had I found him at fault."

"But he decided to leave instead?"

"Aye."

"Then let us go to dinner and celebrate that he is off, relieving you of the responsibility to chastise him." Her stomach chose that moment to rumble loudly.

He grinned and pushed back a few strands of blond hair falling across his eyes. "You state your wishes quite effectively, my lady." He looked down at her and she saw the light of need quicken in his eyes again. "However, if we do not dress anon, we might find ourselves keeping the household overlong from their well-deserved dinner."

Chapter Eleven

The next day Rosalind plunged, once again, into the business of preparing for a crowd of visitors. She barely saw Jeoffrey all day as he spent the morning on the training field, honing his skill with sword and shield. His afternoon was passed with the grooms working out the arrangements for the tents and pavilions their guests would bring and for care of their livestock.

Rosalind dealt first with the dispatch of the goods she'd acquired the previous day, and then with the batch of responses to their invitation that had arrived during her absence. Five more had come, listing family and staff that would be accompanying them and the type of accommodations they'd require. It necessitated a bit of juggling of rooms already assigned, since Sir James Shelton would be requiring quarters within the keep rather than bringing his own pavilion as they'd anticipated. He requested they provide a room with a south window as the breeze from the north didn't agree with his system. Further he would need an additional bed in his room for the attendant he required be with him at all times and extra supplies of water.

When those matters were seen to, she penned messages to two merchants the manor dealt with, suggesting their agreements on certain exchanges of goods would need to be amended. It would help, but… She wasn't sure she wanted to let her thoughts drift that far. However effective her efforts, she doubted she could save enough to equate with the sort of fortune the daughter of the Duke of Barnston could bring.

She checked with the housekeeping staff to ensure the rooms she was counting on for guests would be ready, and informed them of Sir James's particular requirements for his quarter.

With all the necessary business accomplished, she set about the next task. She dreaded facing the group of women of the manor's textile group, but it had to be done. Whatever they might think of her, they would do as she bid in this.

Nonetheless, her palms grew sticky as she went to their workroom. Only four of the five she'd met on her previous venture into their demesne were present. All looked up as she knocked and entered. Not a one of them did more than nod on noting her entrance. The older woman at the spinning machine appeared to be the person in charge, so Rosalind went directly to her though the woman hadn't acknowledged her arrival at all.

"Madame Maressa?" Rosalind ventured. "Did you receive the bolt of silk fabric I sent yesterday with the linen rolls?"

The woman stopped the machine after a moment and looked up, but not directly at Rosalind. "Aye, miss. I did." Her demeanor gave no clue to her thoughts on the subject, but there was no warmth friendliness there.

"Good. I have a plan for that silk and I will need your assistance."

Maressa made no response, just waited, eyes cast down and staring at her thread, for Rosalind to go on. All the other women had halted or slowed their own work and listened to the conversation.

"With the coming convocation of our neighbors, I feel it needful the household, and Lord Jeoffrey, in particular, should make as fine and impressive a show as possible. At his request I have been sorting through his clothing, and I find nothing suitable to this occasion. For that reason I purchased the silk. I have also obtained some lace for trimmings. I would be grateful for your assistance in constructing a new tunic and gambeson for my lord. Have you time, think you?"

Maressa looked up at her suddenly, eyes widening with surprise. Around her, the other women glanced at each other with raised brows and open mouths. It took Rosalind a moment of consideration before she realized they'd all thought the silk was intended to provide a dress for herself and all had put that down as precisely the sort of behavior they expected from person they supposed her to be. They weren't sure how to deal with this turn of events.

The atmosphere in the room changed subtly, becoming not exactly friendly, but less hostile, at least.

"Aye, miss, I believe we can manage to find the time. It would be meet for our lord to have some finer things to show well." Her expression changed to more overt enthusiasm. "He would not put himself out in such a way, but I think we would all be proud to see him the equal of or even overshadowing the others. He could, did he but try a bit. As fine a figure of a man as he is and with the character to back his looks… Yes, we will do it."

Maressa's expression stilled, the enthusiasm departing almost as suddenly as it had arrived "And what of you, Madame?"

"What of me?" Rosalind asked.

"Do you not require better garments for this gathering?"

Rosalind had, of course, given the matter some thought. "I believe not. I am not the lady of the manor, merely my lord's leman, and as such I shall endeavor to remain as quietly unobtrusive as possible. Aside from which…" This was the hard part, the thing she still had difficulty coming to terms with and a problem for which she had, as yet, found no solution. "Many of our guests will know who I am. They will know what… I truly believe it better for everyone if I did not put myself forward overmuch. Better I appear to consider myself more in the line of a poor guest, making the best of bad circumstances."

The women traded glances again, but Rosalind couldn't decipher the meaning of them. Finally Maressa nodded. "Perhaps that would be wise," she murmured. "Now, what had you in mind for our lord?"

For the next half hour they discussed designs for the new clothing, the best way to orient the fabric, cut and trim it. Once the important decisions had been made, Rosalind handed over the lace she'd brought and departed satisfied that Jeoffrey's new garment was in good hands.

As she returned to the office, she encountered Sir Philip coming toward her. A smile lit his handsome face. "Lady Rosalind," he said. "Our lord has just given me the comeuppance of my life on the practice field. Would you take pity on my bruised ego and walk with me in the garden for a bit? Your presence has a soothing effect and I am much in need of calming right now."

She couldn't help but grin at him. "Sir Philip, I suspect you of exaggerating your wounds to win my sympathy. But I would enjoy a turn in the garden in any case."

"Is it that obvious, lady?" he asked, taking her arm and leading her toward the door to the garden.

"I have watched you and my lord together on the field," she said. "You two are nearly evenly matched. That he should best you, I can imagine. That he should give you the 'comeuppance of your life' I take leave to doubt."

"You do indeed provide a soothing balm to my ego."

The weather had turned cooler again and the breeze blew hard with a smell of moisture on it that promised rain. Rosalind hoped it would rain now and clear later, so as not to impede the travel or accommodations of their visitors.

"I understand from Jeoff you have also been an invaluable aid in the preparations for the convocation next week," Sir Philip said.

"I do what I can to assist."

"He tells me most of those invited are planning to attend."

"So it appears," she said.

"Can we accommodate them adequately?"

"'Tis taking our resources near to their end, but, aye, we can manage it."

"That is well. We cannot afford any sign of weakness."

"I appreciate that, Sir Philip. There will be none."

He stopped and smiled at her. "I have no doubt, since the preparations are in your hands."

"Nay, most things are overseen by Jeoffrey's staff. They are very competent and efficient."

Philip nodded. "He chooses who he places in key positions carefully."

"I do not understand, then, why he keeps Ranulf as butler. The man can neither see well nor hear at all."

"Aye. Jeoff's one concession to sentimentality. Ranulf all but raised Jeoffrey. He took pity on the boy who could do no right in his father's eyes, and gave him a father's care and love, encouragement and praise. Jeoff would never deprive Ranulf of his position, no matter how poorly his health fares, nor how much it might interfere with his carrying out his duties. Others watch to ensure no lapses occur."

They walked in silence for a moment, weaving through the kitchen garden to their favorite retreat in the wild garden at the end. The sun broke through the clouds for a moment, warming her.

"But you, my lady," Philip asked. "Are you prepared for this?"

"What mean you, sir?"

"Many of those coming are not strangers to you. Or at least to your family."

She sighed, reached up to pluck a fragrant flower from an early blooming rose, and cradled it in her palm. "Aye, I have given that much thought. All will know what my position is here, and even those who do not will reckon it out with little difficulty. For my lord's sake, I believe it would be best I be seen and heard as little as possible. Should any seek me out to ask, I shall say merely that Lord Jeoffrey rescued me from Sir William's dungeon and this was the reward I offered him, having no other coin with which to pay. It is essentially the truth, and should serve to put him in a good light."

"At the cost of your own reputation."

"Sir Philip, I have none now. And it matters naught. For this effort, Jeoffrey must appear in the best light possible."

"Aye." He stopped to think about the next words for a moment. "My lady, you know that should we succeed in this effort, you might gain much. Perhaps even what you most want."

She glanced at him. "Aye, I had considered the possibility. Should he lead the effort and defeat Sir William, he will gain the resources to protect and provide for his people without need of the duke's daughter's dowry. But the duke may very well make betrothal to his daughter a condition of his assistance."

Philip sighed. "'Tis possible. Has he accepted the invitation?"

"Aye."

"And will his family travel with him?"

"Nay. He comes ahead with a portion of his men. His wife and daughter, who would find the proceedings deadly tedious, will follow after and join us for a visit at the conclusion of the convocation."

"That could work to our benefit. We must find our way to convincing the duke to commit his forces to the effort without the promise of a familial alliance."

She laughed. "I fear, Sir Philip, such an effort is beyond my ability."

"Perhaps not," Sir Phillip said. "But I do not know that it is your task to take on. We shall see how the proceedings go."

"Just so," she answered. "And now I must go attend to my duties. The day is waning."

"And Jeoffrey will be wanting his bath."

"Aye." She hoped the flush that rose at that thought wasn't as obvious to him as it felt to her. In truth, she treasured the time with Jeoffrey, whether they shared a tub or she sat beside him and assisted him. At those times she could tell herself he was entirely hers. She had the freedom of his body, and they frequently passed the time with word games or discussion of the day's events as prelude to more vigorous play.

"Then I shall see you at dinner," Sir Philip said, bowing to her before he departed.

Rosalind took the rose in with her and set it in the basin in the solar she shared with Jeoffrey after she poured a measure of water into it.

She had time to check that an extra cot would be available for Sir James's room and a sheltered spot on the south side of the manor available for the Cottenhams' pavilion before she went to prepare Jeoffrey's bath.

The tub and buckets of hot water awaited him when he came in, walking stiffly and groaning. He tore off his clothes, letting them drop where they would, and climbed into the tub, shifting and stretching his legs to find a comfortable position for them.

"Philip worked me into the ground," he explained to Rosalind as she sat beside the tub and washed him. "Told me I was letting myself get soft. No doubt he is right. Now I feel like a ninety-year-old man."

He had several small bruises on his face and arms, but she suspected most of his discomfort came from muscles not used to the activity he'd put himself though that day.

"Ah." He sighed as he relaxed and let the hot water relieve some of the ache. He kept his eyes open and on her, however. He stopped her hand wielding the rag and held it in his own.

"I asked Elspeth about the preparations of the manor for the visitors. She said that between you two, things were well in hand. I am grateful for all the work you have done to help make this a success."

" I am grateful I am not rotting in Sir William's dungeon. This is little enough to repay."

"Ah, my lady, you have done more than enough to repay that effort already." His smile had a wry curve and it ignited wicked lights in his eyes. "You do so much for me, I feel I should almost thank you for the privilege of having rescued you. You have made me feel things I have never felt before; you make me think new things. When I am with you, holding you in my arms, I feel like more of a man than I ever have before. I believe I can do anything at all."

"My lord, I see not why you need me to make you feel that way. 'Tis nothing but the truth. You are a man among men already."

"So others have said. But only you can make me truly believe it."

"Then know that it is so. I do hereby pronounce it. And will announce it the world do you so desire. But it is so and you must act on it."

His grin turned wry. "Ah, so Sir Philip has been at you. I have seen you walk with him in the garden." The grin disappeared suddenly, and his face grew serious, intent. "Rosalind, do you have feelings for him? Is his the hand you would prefer? It would not be my choice for you, and would not be a pleasant thing for me to have you so near and so untouchable, but if it is what you wish I could arrange it. He is certainly a worthy man."

"Indeed he is, my lord. And he is a very good friend. But no more than that to me. He has no part of my heart, and he deserves better than a wife whose greatest love will always be given elsewhere."

"Rosalind…" He carried her hand to his mouth and kissed it. "You must not think—"

"Shhhh." She put a finger over his lips. "We will not talk of that now. Later it will have to be resolved, and it will. Now is ours." She removed her finger and put her mouth where it had been.

They kissed like two starving people finding a sumptuous banquet set before them, and made love, hard, quick and fierce, before dressing hastily and going down to dinner.

Later they made love again, quieter and longer, never guessing that the next day would bring them to a small crisis in their relationship.

Chapter Twelve

It came early in the day, shortly after they rose, while they were dressing.

Jeoffrey looked at the stack of clothes going down to the laundry since it was midweek-day, then pulled his last clean shirt from the wardrobe. He stuck an arm into it and emitted an incoherent, but decidedly unhappy, grumble.

"Is aught amiss?" Rosalind asked while pulling on her own shift.

"Aye. The shirt feels like a board and scratches like a patch of thorns. I know not why they cannot get my clothes softer. Rosalind, I would like you to take care of doing my laundry yourself," Jeoffrey said. "They always leave my shirts hard, and my hose so stiff they near to stand up on their own."

She stopped and hoped she'd misunderstood. Her heart suddenly pounded. Maybe if she didn't respond, he'd think she hadn't heard and forget about it.

He didn't. "Did you hear?" he asked. "Pray, indulge me and see to my laundry yourself. It would get done the way I would prefer."

"My lord," she said. "I shall be glad to speak to the laundry maids about it and suggest they change the way they do things."

"I have tried it already. One day I get things the way I want, but the next time it is right back to the way it has always been. If you do it, I know it will be right."

"Jeoffrey. I cannot."

"What?" He put down the shirt he was holding and turned to her. "Why not?"

"I cannot. Ask me aught else."

"I need not aught else right now." He frowned. "I need only that you undertake the washing of my things yourself."

"I cannot."

"Why not?"

Her heart raced as she thought about the time Sir William had relegated her to his laundry and the horrible things that had happened there. She'd felt so degraded. But she didn't want anyone to know how low she'd sunk. She couldn't talk about it, even with him. It would make it too *real*. If no one else knew, she could forget it had happened.

"I cannot. Please do not ask it of me."

He stared at her. "Then pray explain why 'tis such a problem. Are you too fine a lady to dirty your hands in that way?"

She drew a couple of hard breaths. "Perhaps so, my lord. There are some things a lady just does not do."

"Even if I ask? Even though you promised me your obedience?"

"My lord—"

"I cannot accept it," he said. "But I will give you the day to reconsider your answer. Know, though, that I cannot let your refusal of a direct request to go unanswered."

As harsh as his words were, something in his expression begged her to accede to his wishes.

"I understand, my lord."

He still stared at he with the pained look. "Rosalind, if there is something I should know or understand, pray tell me."

"I simply cannot do it. That is all," she answered. "Would you punish me before the household for my refusal?"

He considered for a moment. "Nay. This is a private matter between you and me, and does not involve them, so this discipline would be private."

"What would…?"

He looked at her and walked over to the pile of clothes ready to be taken to the laundry. "One stroke of my belt for each item here." He bent down to the pile and counted them. "Eleven things." He straightened up and sighed. "I will ask later whether you chose to do them yourself. I will expect an honest answer."

"And you will get it, my lord," she said. "I hope you know you can depend on that, at least."

He looked at her, saw the plea in her eyes, walked to her and pulled her into his arms. Her cheek brushed against the soft blond hair on his chest. "Aye, I know you will answer me honest." He moved her so that he could look into her eyes while his hands framed her face. "I wish you would answer me differently." He kissed her quickly, then turned, pulled a clean shirt over his head and left the room.

The prospect of having to answer to him later hung over her like a dark cloud for the rest of the day.

It was a day when many small things went wrong. Papers got lost, ink smeared all over one of her diagrams of who was to be placed in which room, the maids came up short on towels for the guest rooms, and another response arrived that necessitated yet another shuffling of room assignations.

To the good side, she received two messages from merchants she'd contacted indicating they'd listen to her proposals on renegotiating their trade agreements.

Once she'd written her replies to those, she fetched Jeoffrey's clothes and her own down to the laundry room. Rosalind had decided she'd see if she could accede to his demands. Perhaps she could do as he wished and handle his laundry herself. But when she walked into the room, the smell and the humidity hit her like an ocean wave, rolling over her until she felt faint and nauseous. She nodded to the women there, dropped her stack of clothing on the pile to be washed and made a hasty exit before she disgraced herself by collapsing on the floor. Dark spots floated across her field of vision.

Once outside the room, she stopped and leaned against the wall, braced by the feel of the cool stone in the basement hallway, until her head cleared enough that she felt she could make it up the stairs. Perspiration felt cold on her skin. She was still shaking by the time she reached the next floor, so she stopped by the kitchen and begged a small measure of wine from the cook to brace and restore her.

She wasn't happy with herself. She didn't like to think she was so weak she couldn't force herself to do a nasty job to fulfill the promise she'd made to Lord Jeoffrey. She dreaded the thought of his punishment. Even more than that, though, she hated to disappoint him in anything. She valued his high regard too much.

The day dragged on.

Dinner took forever, though she was able to eat very little.

Sir Philip teased her about over-working and looking pale but she couldn't bring herself to do anything but agree. Jeoffrey didn't appear to be enjoying himself any more than she was. He sat and glowered at the group, answering questions or comments directed at him but volunteering nothing.

When it was over she followed him to their quarters. Her footsteps were heavy with dread and cold sweat beaded on her chest, making her clothes cling.

He was struggling with a lace on his shirt that had tangled into a knot when she entered the room. His fingers appeared to shake a little.

"Can you get this for me?" he asked.

Her own hands were none too steady as she worked out the knot. She stared at his throat as she worked, admiring the fine lines, firm skin, and graceful play of the muscles there. Once the laces were freed, she stepped back. He put a finger under her chin to raise her face. Their eyes met. In the depths of his she saw love, care, concern, but all held tightly beneath a stern consideration.

"Rosalind? Did you do as I requested this morning and see to the laundering of my things yourself."

Her voice shook as she answered. "Nay, my lord."

"Why not?"

"I… I just could not, my lord. I could not."

"Would you care to explain?"

"Nay. Please my lord… Pray do not ask me again."

"Then you know what must happen next?"

She lowered her head so he would not see the tears starting to form. They owed as much to the expression she saw in his eyes—disappointment, confusion, hurt—as to her dread of punishment. "Aye, my lord."

"Disrobe, then, and stand at the edge of the table."

She removed her clothes, folding them and laying them in a neat pile on the chair. Nude, and oddly embarrassed about it, she walked across the room and stood where indicated by the table.

"Lay forward, across it, and grab the far edge with your hands. Do not let go under any circumstances."

The polished surface of the table was cool and slick against her breasts as they pressed down on it. She saw him retrieve his other belt from the wardrobe and was relieved. The one he'd worn that day had a metal tip on the end. The one he pulled out now was wider, almost four fingers wide, and heavier, being made of two layers of leather sewn together, but it bore no ornaments other than the buckle. She watched him fold the buckle into his hand and let the remaining length swing loose. When he drew his arm back, pulling the strap behind him, she closed her eyes.

"Prepare yourself," he warned.

Moments later she heard the whizzing sound of the strap cutting through the air and then a loud crack as it landed full across her bottom. She stiffened, gasped loudly, and dug her fingers into the wood of the table. The sharp ache of the strike hit her first, but as the leather fell away, leaving its mark, a sizzling burn settled in, spreading fire down her legs and arms. It didn't have the sharp, clawing sting of the birch, but a deeper, harsher ache and burn.

The pain was just starting to settle down when he struck again. It hit higher and harder, drawing a loud sob from her as her body jumped again. She managed to hang onto the edge of the table by locking her fingers in place and refusing to let them release, even when the pain slammed into her and rolled through her in agonizing waves. The tears began to leak from her eyes as she panted and moaned.

The lashes came faster, covering her derriere with fire, then working down along her thighs. Some of the strokes were so hard and sharp, she nearly jumped up and ran. But she hung on and kept hold of the table, though she very much wanted to rub her flaming bottom. The pain grew and grew. Her sobs and moans grew to squeals, then to shrill shrieks and finally to a full scream as the strap slashed across the sore flesh right at the crest of her derriere once again, re-igniting the fire of former strokes and adding its own heat. She writhed frantically and began to plead and beg him to stop, though her words were so broken up by sobs they were barely coherent.

She heard him say, "One more." Then the world exploded in anguish as the strap raked over the same sore area yet again. She screamed. Her body arched into a taut, tense curve as she fought the unbearable pain, then finally fell down on the table again, wriggling frantically.

Then his arms were around her, plucking her from the table. But her fingers were locked so tightly around the edge, he had to pries them gently from their hold, opening them one at a time until she let go. He picked her up and carried her to the bed, where he laid her down on her side. He lay beside her and she rolled over so she could put her face against his chest while she sobbed.

He cradled her gently against him, patting her hair and rubbing her back as she cried and cried. "I am sorry," he said. " I am sorry I had to be so hard on you." When she continued to weep, he said, "Shh... Please... Was it that bad? I am sorry. I did not mean to hurt you that much."

When she finally began to calm somewhat, he moved her so that he could see her face and wiped away the tears remaining on her face. "Did I truly hurt you so much?" he asked. "It was not my intent. I just wanted you to know you could not disobey without consequences."

"Nay, my lord," she said on a long sigh, interrupted by a sobbing hiccup. "It stung, but it did not hurt me *that* much."

"You screamed."

"Aye. For a few minutes, the pain was hot. And my feelings were high. I could not contain it. You did me no great injury, however."

"Why then do you weep so now?"

"I was..." Her voice broke and tears threatened again. He waited while she fought for control. "I was afraid, and I could not bear it."

"Afraid? Of me? Or what I would do?"

"Nay, my lord." She had to swallow hard. "Afraid I had disappointed you. That you would no longer care for me."

Surprise widened his eyes. His arms tightened around her until they threatened to squeeze the breath from her. She didn't complain. It felt wonderful to be held so close and so secure.

"Rosalind, have I not told you the time I have spent with you has been the happiest I have ever known? Think you I would cast you off because one time you defy me? Have you no more faith in me than that?"

"I do not... I do not have the experience to know what to believe. I did promise to obey you, and I failed to keep the promise."

"And accepted the penalty for it," he said. "Rosalind, you did not disappoint me. Surprised me, for certain. Concerned me, because I fear there is more behind this than you are willing to tell me." His smoky gray eyes look dark, shadowed by worry and doubt.

On the side of him where she lay, his hair was darkened by her tears dripping onto it and wetting it. She touched the strands, pushing her fingers into them.

"Aye. There is... My lord, Jeoffrey, I shall try to tell you, but I... I find this hard." Oddly though, when she started to talk, she discovered something about what had happened in the last hour had freed her from the binding imposed by Sir William's attempts to degrade her. "While I was in Sir William's... captivity, he forced me to work in his laundry—as part of his effort to convince me that being his lady would be a more desirable choice."

She went on to describe the conditions there, and the foul treatment she'd received at the hands of the other servants, as ordered, she had no doubt, by Sir William himself. Though she still shuddered remembering it, in the protection of Jeoffrey's arms, she felt safe in admitting it had happened and how it had changed her. While she talked about the degrading things that had passed, a small doubt crossed her mind as to whether he would be repelled on hearing it. Then she recalled his words about trusting him.

"I took your clothes to the laundry myself," she told him. "I told myself it could not truly be so bad and I would be able to do it. But as soon as I smelled and felt the damp air in the room, I grew dizzy. I nearly fainted."

His arms tightened again, drawing her against his body. For a moment the only sound she heard was the noise of his harsh breaths as he fought something that seemed to interfere with the flow of air. "My lady," he said, "Rosalind, I deeply regret what happened to you—at Sir William's hands and at my own." He turned her face up to meet his eyes. "Had I known this earlier, I would have rescinded my request concerning the laundry. Can you believe that?"

She looked into his eyes again, saw the sincerity and the concern. "Aye, Jeoffrey. I know it."

"I will not ask it of you again. And for pity's sake—" He shook her gently. "—next time, explain, if you cannot meet a request I make of you. I will try to understand and I will not force you to actions you feel you cannot manage. Pray, promise me you will do so."

She reached up to trace around his lips, marveling again at how the man filled her heart with emotion until she didn't know how to contain it. "Aye, my lord," she said.

He smiled, warmth and care igniting sparks in his gray eyes. It touched her all the way down to her soul when he looked at her with so much tenderness and love.

His hands stroked down her body to her derriere, where he rubbed carefully, kneading some of the ache and lingering burn from them. Like tinder catching flame, the soreness in her bottom and her spirit turned to heat and longing. Their mouths met and clung to each other, searching fiercely, tongues twining. She worked her hands under his shirt to stroke his chest.

After a few minutes, he disengaged his mouth and carefully turned her onto her back. He watched her face for signs that the pain would be too much, but was satisfied when he saw it wasn't so. He leaned over her and put his lips to her breast, licking the delicate curves, tracing a circle around the tip, and finally closing over the nipple and sucking gently. He switched to the other one after thoroughly tonguing the one. Alternating sides, he swirled, tongued and nipped until she was frantic with longing. When he scraped each tip carefully between his teeth, she screamed and dug her fingers into his hair, letting the silk of it run over her hands, pulling his head down and pinning it against her breast.

He didn't let her hold him there long. Giving her a sly, wicked grin, he slid his mouth down her chest and along her belly. He stopped briefly at her belly button where he poked his tongue in and teased it, then he moved lower, stroking along her abdomen until he reached the joining of her legs.

Using his hands, he pushed her thighs apart. His head dipped down again and this time his tongue slid along the sensitive flesh of her slit, sending shocking waves of pleasure through her body, making her moan and pant.

With tender fingers, he parted the outer lips that guarded her innermost secrets. He stared for a moment at the delicate folds there, then ducked his head again and licked at the most sensitive spot on her body. She shrieked in shock and delight as a spear of purest pleasure lanced through her.

He continued to stroke until she was panting, shaking with a building tension. She buried her fingers in his hair again, but her hands fisted there, holding his head to her. He changed motions of his mouth, beginning to suck her harder and even nipping lightly. Her body tightened like a lute string pulled to its greatest length, then suddenly, it broke, exploded, and her world shattered as waves of ecstasy crested over and drowned her.

He drew back and shifted, holding her while she spasmed repeatedly until her exhausted body could do no more.

When the spasms finally wore themselves out, she turned to him. "My lord, I have never... never known anything like that. It was quite... astonishing. But now—I want you inside me."

From the enormous lump stretching his breeches, she knew he wanted to be there as much as she wanted him. She nearly tore the clothes from his body in her haste to have him bare for her. He wasted no time and moved over her, found his goal, plunged deep into her body. She welcomed his throbbing cock inside her. It stirred the longing again, building a different, deeper kind of tension. He began slowly, however, even when she tried to nudge him along. He plunged and withdrew at his own rhythm, starting so deliberately she nearly screamed with frustration of it. He gradually moved more quickly, stroking harder, until he could no longer contain himself and rocked against her in urgent need. As he approached his climax, she tightened with him, and when he spurted within her, her newly aroused need exploded as well, in another series of bone-jarring spasms.

As they lay together afterwards, spent bodies cuddled close, he said, "Rosalind, my one and only love. You need not be ever perfect for me. I will love you through any faults or wrongs you commit. I love you for your spirit and your honor, your loveliness, your humor, your concern for me and my people, for all the many good things you are and you do." He chuckled lightly. "And for the way you stir my manhood, in truth. No matter how dark and grim things might seem at a time, never doubt that."

" I will try to remember, my lord."

"Jeoffrey," he corrected. "And Rosalind? I hope you can do the same for me. I am far from perfect myself, and there will be mistakes. I hope you can love me through those as well."

"Always, my dear. Whatever the future holds for us, I will love you always."

He sighed deeply and wrapped his arms around her, holding her like she was the most precious thing in the world to him. She hoped it was so.

As the time for the guests to arrive drew near, the affairs of the manor grew into activity so frenzied, it sometimes appeared not far removed from complete chaos. But Rosalind knew better. Each person had his or her job and did it as efficiently as possible. She watched carefully, giving subtle direction or lending assistance as needed. When two of the housemaids became ill for a day, Rosalind helped with the cleaning and scrubbing herself.

When Elspeth had to decide how to distribute basins and ewers and chamberpots, she consulted Rosalind for advice. The two women together assessed what they had and how best to dispose of them. An unexpected understanding arose between them as they found they had similar thoughts on many issues and approached problems the same way.

She checked with the ladies in the textiles room. Lord Jeoffrey's new clothes progressed well. One of the younger women had a remarkable talent for decorative embroidery. The border she'd created for the gambeson was both cleverly designed and beautifully executed. They were nearly ready for Jeoffrey himself to come for a final fitting. Rosalind promised to get him there.

The women were noticeably more friendly now than on previous occasions and even went so far as to smile, share jests, and speculate about the coming guests. Two of the young ladies were unmarried, and the others teased them about seeking possible mates in the throng.

Though none mentioned it, Rosalind strongly suspected Jeoffrey would be using the occasion to attempt to arrange a suitable marriage for her as well. The thought made her want to run away and hide herself out of view until it was over and the danger that she might be handed over to another man past.

One of the greatest surprises of her life came two days before the first of the guests had indicated they'd be arriving. She was in Lord Jeoffrey's office, working on the final list of guests and seating arrangements for mealtimes. A knock at the door preceded the entrance of all the upper staff: Ranulf, Elspeth, Brenna, Ferris, and Maressa. The group stopped and waited awkwardly for Ferris to step forward and speak.

"My lord?" he asked. "We've been consulting among ourselves," he said, indicating the gathered group. "We have a request to bring to you."

"Aye?"

"You may not appreciate it, my lord." Ferris warned.

Jeoffrey's mouth crooked in a wry smile. "I'd guessed from your reluctance to meet my eyes such might be the case."

"Aye." Ferris coughed gently and began again. "We have consulted and we wish to respectfully put our request before you."

"Proceed," Jeoffrey invited him.

Ferris looked dubiously toward Rosalind then faced Lord Jeoffrey again. "We would like to suggest that Lady Rosalind move from your quarters."

Chapter Thirteen

Rosalind could barely contain her astonishment, but she let Jeoffrey answer.

"I do not believe our living arrangements are your concern."

Ferris drew a deep breath. "We believe they are, my lord, and we hope you will listen to our reasons."

Jeoffrey rolled his eyes. His wry grin deepened, showing the wickedly attractive groove in his cheek. "You know very well I will listen. You shall ensure my life is unbearable until I do so. Proceed. And I hope your reasons are good ones."

"I hope my lord will agree they are," Ferris answered with little change of inflection. "We have discussed this at some length and we are in agreement. With the coming assemblage of our neighbors and allies, it is most important that you, my lord, be perceived as a host above reproach. Much depends on the outcome of this assembly. Many of those coming will know the Lady Rosalind and will be curious about her position here. We believe it will serve best if the lady be seen to be an honored guest in your household, one who is treated with utmost dignity and respect. Lady Rosalind must move to a solar of her own. We have a room in mind. 'Tis gracious and comfortable enough for a lady, yet somewhat too small to be suitable for any of our guests and is far enough away from your quarters to be above suspicion. In addition, we'd like to suggest you allow her to function as your hostess for the occasion. We are confident she can carry the role with grace."

"I trust you are not implying I have ever treated Lady Rosalind with anything other than the respect she deserves."

Ferris coughed gently. "Of course not, my lord. We are talking about how the situation will be seen by others outside our household, not what we know to be the truth. We have already spoken with our respective staffs to ensure there will be no gossip or loose talk while our guests are in residence."

"I see," Jeoffrey said. He folded his hands into a tent on the table, weaving his fingers together, and supported his chin on them while he considered their request. His gray eyes darkened in thought. The gathered servants began to look at each other and a couple shifted nervously.

Jeoffrey lifted his head and gave a long sigh. "Perhaps you are right." He looked at Rosalind with resignation and apology. "It *would* be better for Lady Rosalind to have a private solar well away from mine. Are you agreeable, my lady?"

She wanted to protest, but she knew the servants were right about how her position would be perceived and the possibly negative effects it might have on Jeoffrey's ability to bring their guests to a consensus for action. "Aye, my lord. But in the matter of acting the hostess, I do foresee a few difficulties."

"Such as?"

"Perhaps most important, I have not the wardrobe for such a role. I have only the garments you have provided, and while they have been more than adequate for my functions heretofore, they are by no means appropriate for the role of hostess to this assemblage."

Madame Maressa spoke up then. "We have considered that, too, my lady. While 'tis a pity we do not have the time and fabric to make more suitable things, there is a trunk of clothes that belonged to our late lady, my lord's mother. She was not so different in size from you and she had some grand gowns. With my lord's permission, we can make over some of her things to fit you."

"It appears you have this well planned out," Lord Jeoffrey said.

Ferris coughed again. "We have discussed it at some length."

"Obviously. Have you any other suggestions for ordering my life to better suit your purposes?"

"I believe the rest can be safely left in your hands, my lord," Ferris said.

"Very well," Jeoffrey conceded. "Move her to... Where are you suggesting Lady Rosalind take up residence?"

"There is a small room in the south tower, my lord. 'Tis small but comfortable. We had thought to use it for Sir Andrew Connington, but he travels with a servant he wants to keep close, and it would not be suitable."

"And 'tis as far away from my quarters as you can get and still be within these walls," Jeoffrey commented.

Ferris's expression did not change, though most of the others grinned.

"Aye, it is, my lord. The better to avert loose talk."

"Indeed." He stood up. "You have had your way. Go, now, and get back to your own work and leave me to do mine."

"Aye, my lord. And thank you for listening to us."

Jeoffrey feigned surprise. "I had a choice?"

For the first time Ferris looked disconcerted. "My lord is always the final authority in such things."

Jeoffrey shook his head and made a vain attempt to look stern. "As long as I do as you wish."

"Good day, my lord." Ferris turned to leave and the others followed him out.

Rosalind stood also and addressed Elspeth. "I will consult with you shortly concerning moving my things."

The housekeeper nodded and left with the others.

When they had departed and the door was shut behind them, Jeoffrey came to her and embraced her. "This is not what I would have wished. But perhaps it is for the best. 'Tis selfish of me to want to keep you with me at all times."

"'Tis not my desire either. But perhaps 'tis better we begin to get used to being apart. We will have to part in truth soon enough anyway."

"Aye. But not yet. For now, you are still mine. No one said I cannot come visit you in the dead of night when everyone should be fast abed."

"As long as you are very discreet about it, my lord."

Jeoffrey laughed heartily. "Discreet? There will likely be a crowd going stealthily from one room to another."

"Perhaps so," she admitted. "Oh. I hope I have not put the wrong people too close together."

"Worry not about it. Who wishes to see whom will change from day to day in any case. Save that I will always be making my way to your side."

She wrapped her arms around him and pressed into his body. She sank into the feel of his strong arms holding her, the rhythmic beat of his heart, the strength of the shoulder her face rested on, the soft, silky slide of his loose hair against her cheek, the smell of leather, horses, soap and something just basically masculine about him. She'd never imagined feeling such possessive desire for another person and wondered how she'd ever be able to adjust to a life that didn't include him.

He sat in the one chair in the room and drew her onto his lap. After releasing the tapes holding her clothes on, he pulled them off her shoulders and let them drop to puddle around her waist. His fingers sought her breasts. He caressed gently, circling the tips often. He watched her face as he touched, reading her delight and excitement.

He worked his hands down her body, leaving trails of warm, tingling skin as he went. He pushed the fabric further down her body to have access to her belly and then below. Finally he moved her enough to pull all the clothing off and toss it aside.

His mouth and hands began a slow, sensuous assault on her body that built the heat to flaming point and beyond. Then he stood with her in his arms and carried her to the bed. Instead of laying her on her back, he rolled her over until she was face down.

He ran his hands down her back in a light massage that stirred every inch of skin into life and awareness. Then he moved down and stroked her buttocks, slapped them lightly and brushed along the crack. His finger probed in the various openings until she moaned softly and reached for him.

She rubbed along his thighs and up to his balls. She tugged at the edges of his hose, pulling open the lacings until they slid down his legs, and ran her fingers along the hard shaft until he drew a sharp breath and his hand stilled momentarily.

He climbed up on the bed beside her and lifted her without turning her until she was on her hands and knees. Before she understood what he was about, he crouched over her and began to enter her from behind.

The different angle brought a new feeling in her belly, a strange sort of filling that still satisfied. While he supported his weight on one arm, with the other he reached under and around her until he was able to cup her breast and tease the tip. His balls slapped softly against her slit each time he pushed into her. The combination of sweet torments sent her over the edge into spasms of ecstasy. He spilled his seed shortly thereafter, shuddering and panting.

They collapsed together and ended up on their sides, facing each other, limbs entwined. He wrapped his arms around her and pulled her close against him while he whispered in her ear.

"You constantly amaze me. I know not how I shall sleep without you here. You bring me a peace and contentment I have never known."

"I will find sleeping alone difficult as well," she answered.

She hated to let anything steal these last few precious hours of togetherness from them, but eventually she succumbed to drowsiness.

The next day, the last before the first of their guests were due to arrive, Elspeth and Glennys helped her move her few things into her new quarters. The room was small, but comfortably furnished. A low fire crackled merrily in the fireplace to take the chill off the area, and fresh linens had been supplied. Rosalind could not say for certain, but she suspected the velvet drapes with their silk tassels and the linen bed hangings edged in lace were newly installed. A settee upholstered in velvet matching the drapes and a cherry-wood wardrobe and dresser made it a solar fit for a grander lady than she. The window had a lovely view over the gardens at the side of the manor, with a river in the distance.

Still, for all the beauty of the decorations and richness of the furnishings, it felt empty to her. In just the few short weeks she'd been here, she'd grown used to Jeoffrey's company and the way he seemed to fill a room just by entering it.

She had little time to brood on it, however. There was much to do, ascertaining all quarters were ready and everyone's specific requirements would be met, helping with last-minute cleaning and working out the details of meals for the following days. Plus she had to drag Jeoffrey down to the sewing area to try the fit of the new garments, and then remain herself to try on the clothes the ladies had altered for her. As they'd guessed, little actually needed to be done other than a tuck here and there.

She expected to fall asleep quickly that night, but instead she rolled and turned. Lying in the grand bed, which was large enough to accommodate two, the loneliness almost overwhelmed her. For a long time she remained awake, restless and unable to get comfortable, but then she dozed off. She thought at first it was a dream when she heard the soft knock at her door in the small hours of the morning, but then it creaked open and Jeoffrey, in a robe and bare feet, came tiptoeing in to join her. She couldn't stifle her giggles as he climbed into her bed, though the feel of his cold flesh did cause her to flinch away for a moment.

"You are naughty, my lord," she told him, between kisses. "If the servants find you creeping about like this where you do not belong, they may demand you be punished."

"I shall not accept it," he said. "I am still lord here and the decision on who belongs where is mine. I agreed with them that appearances dictated you move to these quarters. I never said I would confine myself to my own for the nights."

She started to answer but he touched her where she most loved it and the intense pleasure stole her voice and any will to protest.

They lay, bodies twined together, in the afterglow enjoying the peace of fulfillment. She rejoiced in just having him close, touching him, being enclosed in his arms and held next to his warm body. She knew their time was brief, and all too soon, he reluctantly kissed her goodbye and returned to his own quarters.

After he'd left, she speculated for a while about the convocation that would begin arriving the next day and the implications it might have for their future.

Chapter Fourteen

The first of the guests arrived just after midday. Rosalind thought activity had been frantic for the past couple of weeks, but it rose to a level several times beyond what had gone before once the visitors began to flood in. Their own staff was swelled many times by the addition of servants and aides accompanying the lords, barons and knights, which meant a surge in requests, demands, accidents and summonses. Special requests that hadn't been mentioned before became urgent needs. Rosalind and the entire staff were kept running in the effort to satisfy all.

She was also called frequently to the gates to greet guests as they arrived, since she was acting as hostess. It was an awkward business when she had no official standing in the household. To those who didn't already know her, Lord Jeoffrey introduced her as Lady Rosalind Hamilton, whom he'd rescued from Sir William de Railles's dungeon and to whom he'd offered the shelter and protection of his household until such time as her future was settled.

Though most had known her family, or at least known of them, nearly all the guests were surprised by her survival. Some, noting the current circumstances, greeted her with cool civility. In Lord Jeoffrey's presence none dared snub her entirely. More, however, showed her an effusive warmth.

One or two of her father's old friends were both surprised and delighted to see her. Sir John of Carbreath expressed a general belief that she'd been killed along with the rest of her family in Sir William's siege. Rosalind was surprised and moved to see tears in the old man's eyes as he kissed her cheeks and told her how very pleased he was to know she'd survived. He turned to Lord Jeoffrey to thank him for his efforts in rescuing her.

The Earl of Dunwood was equally pleased to see her, bowing over her hand as she curtsied to him, but Lady Dunwood was much more reserved in her enthusiasm. The countess nodded politely but said only the minimum courtesy demanded. The ladies who accompanied their lords and fathers were generally more skeptical and cautious in their greetings than the men.

Looking on Lord Jeoffrey, she could well understand why they might be dubious. Her lord wore a plain shirt, tunic, leggings, and boots, saving the grander clothes for later, but he carried himself with an air of nobility that eclipsed most of the knights, baronets, and even the two earls he greeted. He was taller than all but one or two, younger than most, and more handsome than any of them. Beyond that, though, he had a presence, a stature, a confident way of holding himself that added depth and weight to his nobility. The men all smiled and greeted him with affectionate respect. The ladies simpered or smoldered and eyed him with predatory speculation.

Several of the men—single and wed, but more of the bachelors—kissed her hand and bowed while taking careful inventory of her physical assets. To a man, all appeared pleased by what they saw and a few openly teased or flirted as they greeted her. Rosalind suspected Jeoffrey had already put out word he sought a husband for her.

By dinner time, she felt ready to fall into bed and sleep, no matter who else was or wasn't there with her. Instead she freshened up quickly and dressed in one of the new gowns for the evening's entertainment. The musicians she had engaged to perform that evening were a local group, but a well-known bard, hearing of the coming convocation, had also arrived. Before proceeding to the great hall, she checked with the cook and majordomo to be sure all was in order. This wasn't the largest or most important meal to be served. The next day's midday meal, when all should be gathered and the deliberations about to begin, and the dinner following that, hopefully celebrating a consensus and plan of action, would be more significant, but a good start this evening would help relieve anxieties and set a positive tone for the days to come.

She met Jeoffrey on the stairs as she went down to the kitchens. After a quick peek in either direction to ascertain they were alone, he drew her into his arms and kissed her until she felt her bones melt. She ran her hands into his hair and pinned his mouth to hers. His clever tongue and lips stroked and prodded, rousing an irresistible hunger.

He drew her up a few steps and off to the side, into an alcove dimly lit by just one high, narrow window. He fumbled the gown aside enough so he could stroke her breasts as he continued to work his mouth on hers. She felt his cock rise and she fumbled at the laces of his hose to free it. He lifted her onto a rough, wood table, pushed her gown and shift up and out of the way, stripped away her drawers, and parted her legs.

He had to crouch a bit to fit his cock into her, until she rose so she was standing on a cross-bar support of the table. He held her steady as he pumped into her. She moaned when desire rose and filled her, responding to his invasion. The heat sent perspiration down her body. Despite her awkward pose, she moved in rhythm with him, following his pace as it increased. They climaxed together, smothering their screams in each other's mouths.

He held her as close against him as he could for a while.

"Rosalind, my dear, my only love," he whispered in her ear. "Stolen moments with you are not enough. I will never get enough of you and your sweetness." He drew a deep breath, sighed and added, "I suppose I must let you go now. Our guests await."

"Aye, Jeoffrey. Now, though, I will carry the scent and feel of your love with me for the remainder of the evening."

He helped her rearrange her clothes, then disappeared back up the stairs while she proceeded on down them.

Though the kitchens might appear to be in a state of utter chaos to a stranger's eye, Rosalind had learned enough of its workings to realize preparations were in good order. Cook nodded to her when Rosalind leaned in to see if anything was needed, indicating all was well.

Rosalind had never played hostess at an affair of this type before. She had, once or twice, entertained a few of her father's friends or relatives when her mother was indisposed. But her mother had been acknowledged a splendid hostess, and Rosalind had learned from her. She made her way through the hall, stopping to talk with each person or group, inquiring about their journey and whether the accommodations were comfortable.

Those who knew her, and a few who didn't but had heard of her family's tragedy, sought more details of how she'd come to be in Lord Jeoffrey's home. She offered the short version—that she had happened to be among a group of prisoners Lord Jeoffrey had rescued from Sir William's dungeon, but unlike the others she had no family or home to return to, so he had generously offered her his protection until her future could be settled. It was the truth, if not the entire truth, but it served and satisfied those who inquired.

As the time for the meal to start drew near, Rosalind escorted various guests to their places at the tables.

She'd had a long discussion with Elspeth concerning where to place herself. As hostess, she should be at Jeoffrey's right side, but that position would also imply more about their relationship than was wise. After discussing a number of possibilities, they decided to place the Earl of Dunwood at Jeoffrey's right, then the countess, Sir James Shelton and Lady Shelton beyond them, and finally herself on the end of the head table. That put her on the corner, which was a convenient location for someone who might have to rise occasionally to see to the guests' comfort or check with the kitchen.

As Jeoffrey took his seat, Rosalind felt her palms grow sticky and her breathing get a little faster. She hadn't anticipated she'd feel so nervous about this event, but she couldn't help worrying something might go disastrously wrong and blight their gathering. The group grew quiet when Jeoffrey stood to welcome everyone. His speech was short but appeared to impress his guests, though perhaps more for his bearing and the way he projected his voice through the room with the authority of a king.

"Welcome, my friends and neighbors. I rejoice to see each and every one of you here this evening. Though we come together in troubled times, for this evening let no shadow hang over us. I declare: tonight we celebrate the good fortune in our fellowship and respect for each other. The Lord be with us as we break bread and share cups. My good lords and gentle ladies, I drink to your good health and good fortune."

He sat down amidst applause and exclamations. The servants brought in platters loaded with cured fish, capon, blanc-mange, and several haunches of pork. Bowls of greens drenched in herbed vinegar, boiled tubers and stewed apples were passed around. Baskets of bread emitted mouth-watering aromas.

Once they began to eat, Lady James Shelton leaned over toward her. "Lady Rosalind, your mother was once a good friend to myself and my husband. We were grieved to hear of your family's tragedy, then unexpectedly elated to learn you had survived, though not without enduring some terrible trials."

"I was very fortunate, my lady," Rosalind admitted, reassured by the woman's pleasantly sympathetic tone. "My rescue was almost by accident since those who saved me from the dungeon initially had no idea I was there." She glanced toward Jeoffrey, who laughed at something the earl said to him. As though feeling her regard, he looked over toward her and their eyes met briefly. The unspoken communication warmed her with its message of pride and approval.

"Please, call me Jane, if you will, Rosalind. You are perhaps doubly fortunate to have come under Lord Jeoffrey's protection," Jane said. "He is a good and honorable man." She gave Rosalind a wry grin. "And a very handsome one, too."

"Aye, he is that," Rosalind admitted.

"And unmarried." Jane's look was shrewd but not unkind. "As are you." The woman saw Rosalind's reaction and said quickly, "Nay, pray forgive me, Rosalind, I meant no suggestion of impropriety. I meant only that there appears to be some... affection between the two of you, and I wondered if there might be a betrothal in the offing." The warm concern in her tone made Rosalind feel she could like this woman, who appeared to be about ten years older than herself.

"I fear there is not," Rosalind said. "There are circumstances that make it difficult. My position is not what it was. My family's lands and chattels are now in Sir William's possession."

"Ah, and Lord Jeoffrey's in need of a bride with good connections. Has he someone in mind?"

"Aye. Lady Alys."

"The duke's daughter? He aspires high." She looked at Jeoffrey and then back to Rosalind. "But not well. The girl is rumored to be a willful, vain, self-centered brat."

"But she is well dowered," Rosalind pointed out.

"Especially well dowered, I have heard, since her father yearns to have her become someone else's problem. She disrupts the household with tantrums and pouts when crossed. Jeoffrey would have his hand full with her."

Rosalind thought about that and wondered how the girl would react to the household discipline of the manor should she indeed be wed to Jeoffrey. "I believe the lady favors his suit, but the duke hesitates over the match since Jeoffrey is a rather minor lord."

"I am sure she favors it," Jane said. "Jeoffrey is the handsomest man around. 'Twould suit her vanity well enough to have him." She sighed and shook her head. "He's also one of the strongest and most honorable. It would be great sport to watch the two of them together." She laughed. "I know not who I would wager to win the wars of wills between them." Jane took a long sip of spiced wine. "But what about yourself, my dear? Are there any prospects in view?"

"Lord Jeoffrey has said he would undertake to help make an arrangement for me. I believe he means to use this gathering to consider suitable prospects. You know most of these people, Jane. Tell me which of the gentlemen here would make a good match for me," Rosalind asked.

Jane scanned the room, her gaze lighting occasionally on one or the other of the men present, before she turned back to Rosalind.

"None of them," she said.

"Not a one? Surely there must be a few unwed gentlemen here."

"Oh, there are," Jane said, "but none would be suitable for you."

She nodded toward an elderly man hunched over the table opposite them, spooning food into his mouth as fast as he could shovel. Not all of it remained in his mouth, unfortunately, due to the lack of a dental barrier preventing its escape.

"Lord Michel de Granfel seeks a wife, " Jane said, "Though it surely cannot be for anything more than to have someone bring him warm milk and tuck him into bed at night." She tapped her cup with her fingernails and a mocking smile crooked her mouth "Nay, I take back my previous words. He might be just the match for you."

Rosalind stared at her.

"My dear, do you not see? Lord Michel has a nice fortune, and at most a few more years left in this world to enjoy it. His son will inherit, but someone as clever as you could easily ensure you are well-provisioned for widowhood."

"I do not think—"

Jane shook her head and gestured subtly at another, very large young man sitting halfway down a side table. "Do you prefer someone rather younger? There is Sir Arnor. He is a third son, unfortunately, and rumored to be rather slow and simple, but look at his size! And he is said to be good with sword and bow. Still, he will have little fortune of his own, and I doubt even someone with your gifts could manage him into much ambition."

"But one suspects his size could be a gift of a different sort to the right lady," Rosalind commented.

"My dear, what a very shocking thing to say." Jane turned and gave her a look of feigned horror before a giggle escaped. The mischievous sparkle in her eyes had already belied her words "No doubt 'tis true. Still he is not for you. You need a man with some means and intelligence enough to keep you from death by boredom."

"Oh, there is Sir Bartram." Rosalind followed Jane's line of sight to a middle-aged man with graying black hair and a wild, gray-streaked beard.

"He is reputedly in search of another wife, having used up two previous ones. He needs a mother for his six children and someone to satisfy his notoriously prodigious appetites. His holdings are modest but enough to maintain him in some comfort."

"He's not a horrible-looking man," Rosalind commented.

"No. Just a horrible-tempered one. He is said to treat his wives, children, servants, and anyone else weaker than him with shameful brutality. Rumor even suggests one of his wives died at his hand."

"You do not encourage me much," Rosalind said. She glanced around the room, more to be sure all was in order and no one being neglected than in consideration of potential mates. Sir Philip looked her way as her gaze scanned over his position. He smiled and tipped his cup ever so slightly in her direction.

Jane saw the motion and interpreted it correctly. "Hmm, now that is a possibility, especially if this enterprise we presume Jeoffrey plans goes well. One has to believe that if they can defeat Sir William, Jeoffrey will ensure his friend benefits."

"But if it does go well—" Rosalind let her gaze rest on Jeoffrey for just a moment, taking in how handsome and noble he looked even while conversing with a rather deaf lord seated to his left.

Again Jane followed her glance and drew conclusions. "Ah, of course," she said. "So that is your hope. And if the enterprise goes well... Aye, of course it would be so. And quite appropriate, too. Does he know of this secret hope of yours? No, obviously not, if he continues to plan a betrothal with Lady Alys. Yet, you two would be well matched. In fact, I cannot imagine how two such attractive people could be living under one roof and not be tempted to— Oh."

Rosalind did not think her expression had changed, but she felt the heat flooding her cheeks, so perhaps that was what Jane saw. "Nay, 'tis not as you think."

"And you are sure you know what I think?" Jane asked.

"Others have speculated on it. I doubt it could be avoided since I have no one to chaperone me here."

"And what better sport have we than to speculate on who is sinning with whom?" Jane suggested. "But fascinating though the subject might be, at the moment, I am more interested in what your hearts and minds are doing than in your bodies' interactions."

"Then you are the only in this room. Perhaps the only one in this land."

"I pride myself on not doing what everyone else around me is doing," Jane answered.

Rosalind knew for a certainty she was going to like this lady very much.

"So," Jane continued. "Has he given you any reason to hope his deeds might not follow his words?"

The servants were collecting empty trenchers and setting out platters of cheese, fruit and cook's delectable honey rolls. While she watched them work, Rosalind debated the wisdom of answering the question. "As he is trying to arrange marriages for himself and me with others, it would not be wise for him to display any affection elsewhere."

Jane laughed softly. "A careful answer, Rosalind, and a wise one. You know not you can trust me as yet." She took another drink of wine, and then asked, "Is the duke coming to this meeting?"

"Aye, tomorrow."

"And will his wife and daughter be with him?"

"Not immediately. They will arrive afterward and stay for a few days' visit."

"Is the marriage a condition of his assistance?"

"We know not. The duke does not entirely favor my lord, but his daughter does, and you have already said how effective she is at getting what she wants."

"Well. We have some work to be about on the duke, do we not, Rosalind?"

Rosalind turned to stare at the other woman. "My lady, Jane, why would you seek to help me?"

"I said earlier, your mother was a friend to us when we needed one. And, in truth, I like you, Lady Rosalind. I like Lord Jeoffrey as well, and I think you two well matched. Your happiness would please me."

"Then I think we must bend all our efforts toward ensuring my lord gets the support he needs for the venture he proposes. All our hopes of happiness and peace, likely even of survival, rest on that."

"You truly believe Sir William covets all the land around?"

"I spent considerable time with him, listening to him try to woo me with his plans and ambitions. Aye, I know it to be true. And he is not a man to listen to the voice of reason from any other quarter. He consults only his own greed and ambition."

Jane's expression turned serious. "That agrees with my own impression, formed merely from what I had heard of the man. And I believe Lord Jeoffrey may be the only one who can bring together the majority of the lords in the area. He is a leader all would follow. Well, then, we shall make it our business to win support for him." She set down the piece of apple she'd picked up and her solemn expression grew darker. "Tell me how your family died. I know 'tis not a pleasant memory to recall, especially at a feast such as this, but we must be sure 'tis known by all."

Rosalind's stomach turned over and for a moment she wasn't sure her dinner would remain in her middle. She understood the wisdom of Jane's request, however. Only she survived to tell the world of how her family was butchered. She related the story to Jane, leaving out nothing, not even what she'd heard of her mother's dishonor.

The other woman looked rather sick when she finished as well, but she nodded and took Rosalind's hand. "My dear, how horrible for you. I expected it to be bad, but I had not guessed it would be so barbaric. This must not remain secret. As difficult as it will be for you, all must know how your family was treated at Sir William's hands. We have little time to spread the news before they meet tomorrow. Perhaps…"

"What?"

"Think you Lord Jeoffrey might permit you to address the assembly? To tell your story directly to them? It would be most effective, I believe. You tell it with power and emotion that could not fail to move them."

"But would they not be shocked by the impropriety of it?"

"Not if you can convince Jeoffrey to insist upon it."

Chapter Fifteen

The meal went on for a long time. After the food was consumed, people remained to drink and talk. The bard performed for a couple of hours, singing many old favorites and a few new compositions of his own. His musicianship was superb and he was an excellent storyteller as well, so he kept the group entertained for the entire time.

Towards evening's end, Rosalind grew so tired she could barely keep her feet under her, but she dutifully waited near the exit of the hall to bid goodnight to guests and ensure all could find their way to their quarters and had everything they needed. Jeoffrey also remained, talking to a couple of the men in a way that suggested he was trying to convince them of something and not being entirely successful.

When only she and the group of men remained, Jeoffrey bade them all good evening, excused himself, and made his way to her side. He took her hand and kissed her cheek.

"My lady, you did a superb job of organizing the affair this evening. Everyone has remarked on how wonderful the food and entertainment were. I am deeply grateful for your efforts."

"It was my pleasure, my lord," she said, mindful of the men who could see and possibly hear what they said to each other. "'Tis the least I can do to repay all the kindness you have shown me."

"Would you accompany me a moment?" he asked. "There is a problem I need to discuss with you."

She nodded and walked with him out the exit and down the hall to his private office area. When they were in private, he pulled her to him and kissed her more deeply. "I am truly grateful," he said, when they finally came up for air.

"Did it go well, think you?" she asked. "Will they do as you wish?"

He grimaced. "I cannot say yet. Some of those I consulted this evening are hesitant. Not all believe the threat Sir William represents to them."

"My lord, if I might make a suggestion?" She hesitated, knowing he might not approve, and even if he did, what she offered filled her with dread.

"I am listening."

"With your permission—I would like to address your assembly tomorrow. I am aware 'tis of questionable propriety, and it will not be easy for me, but I think if they hear my story, know what was done to my family, and learn what Sir William told me of his ambitions, they might be more inclined to agree with your plans."

He hesitated, weighing her arguments for a moment, then nodded. "Aye. If you think you have it in you to do this, it might help."

"Jane—Lady Shelton thought so also."

He smiled. "I saw you two were deep into plans and calculations."

"She was a friend to my parents, and seems inclined to be one to myself as well. She is also of our mind concerning Sir William. I think she will prove a useful ally."

"She might indeed," he said.

A huge yawn overwhelmed Rosalind at that moment.

Jeoffrey smiled and said, "Be off to your bed. We'll have an early start to a busy morning. This night… Nay, I will not come to your bed this night. We both have more need of rest. But know you'll be in my thoughts and dreams, and I will ache for not having you in my arms. Tomorrow we will talk more."

He kissed her once more before he gently turned her toward the door.

She had thought she'd miss his presence, and she did, but only very briefly. Exhaustion claimed her and took her off to sleep soon after she lay down.

Glennys came early to her quarters the next morning to wake her, bearing a cup of warmed cider, bread and jam. Servers were already beginning to haul platters of rolls, toasted bread, pots of honey and jam, and trays of cheese and sliced cold meats to the great hall by the time she got there.

A few early-rising guests had already arrived. Two ladies picked daintily at rolls while another man had already heaped a trencher high and was digging into it with earnest effort.

Rosalind talked with each, ascertaining all had what they needed and had slept well, and greeted others as they arrived.

Shortly thereafter Jeoffrey entered the room. Though she faced away from the door, she knew something had occurred when conversations trailed off suddenly and the room quieted. She turned. He wore the new clothes she'd had prepared for him, and he looked grand enough to rival any duke or king. The tunic had been cut and fitted to cling closely to his long, lean frame, but it emphasized his broad shoulders. The deep blue color was a brilliant foil for his blond hair and emphasized the sparkle of his gray eyes.

He made his way directly to her, though he sent greetings to all present as he went. "My lady," he said, taking her hand. "I trust you rested well?"

"I did, thank you. And I hope my lord did so, also?"

"Well enough, if not long enough," he said. "But you are looking very well this morning."

"Thank you, my lord." She felt like an actor in a play as she exchanged the banal words with Jeoffrey and curtseyed to him, when she desperately wanted to throw herself on him and kiss him until they neither one could think straight.

He turned away, to give his attention to his guests, and another very busy day began.

The Duke of Barnston arrived at midmorning. His considerable entourage included the carriage he rode in, a dozen mounted knights, a cart with his pavilion and thirty or more servants. The duke himself was a man of just over middle height and middle years, but still straight and trim. He had iron gray hair under his fanciful chaperone, a multi-layered fall of fabric from a rounded crown. His expression remained severe as he alighted from the carriage, until he caught sight of Jeoffrey, and his face softened into something not quite a smile but at least friendlier.

Jeoffrey bowed and welcomed him, then escorted him to Rosalind, where he introduced her. She made her courtesy to the duke, who nodded and said, "Ah, yes, I had heard of the fate of your family. A terrible sorrow to you, my lady."

"Thank you, your grace," she answered.

The duke nodded and accompanied Jeoffrey into the great hall, where he refreshed himself with food and ale.

Lady Shelton again sat next to her for the midday meal, a simpler affair than the previous night's dinner, but still more elaborate than their norm due to the number of people present and the high rank of so many of them.

"I understand from Jeoffrey you will be addressing the group," Jane said to her, once the formalities of the meal had been completed and folks dipped into the food.

"Aye, but I confess I do not know if I can manage it. My hands are shaking already as I think about it."

"Tell it to them as you told it to me yesterday," Jane advised. "Pretend you are relating the story to a friend. If you feel very nervous, choose one friendly face in the crowd and tell your story to him."

Rosalind thanked her for the advice and tried to relax. Later she couldn't remember what she ate, or even if she did eat. Nor could she remember what she and Jane discussed, though she knew they'd chatted through most of the meal. Or rather, Jane chatted. Rosalind listened and tried to pay attention. She did remember to ask the other woman if she would lead the ladies outside for recreation on the lawn after the meal, and keep them organized until she could get away. Jane immediately agreed.

Fortunately the weather favored them with bright sunshine and warm temperatures. Rosalind longed to be going out-of-doors with the other ladies rather than facing the gathered group of men and reciting the horrible memories she carried within. As the lords, knights, and gentlemen congregated closer to the head tables, where Jeoffrey stood and called them to order, she tried to rehearse the lines she'd speak. Her heart pounded in her chest and sweat made her smock stick to her body.

After reviewing the notice he'd received a fortnight prior concerning Sir Williams' latest depredations, Jeoffrey invited her to come stand beside him and relate her story to the men.

Her voice wavered as she began by speaking of her father, mother, and brother, their peaceful existence and the way they had always tried to do the right thing by friends, neighbors and vassals. Most of her nervousness fled as she spoke of the terrible day, how they'd awakened to the alarm of the approaching soldiers, and then the nightmare that ensued. Anger and outrage strengthened her as she related the way her family had died and she'd been carried off by Sir William. She spoke only briefly of her subsequent treatment at his hands, but mentioned how the man had bragged of his ambitions to own this entire corner of the country.

"Your grace, my lords, gentlemen," she concluded, "I tell all of this not to ask for your sympathy or to spread gloom and despair; but only to warn you of Sir William's ambitions and his cruelty. My family was in the path of his ambition and paid a dear price for it. Though you may not be as close as some, all of your families stand in peril of his ambition as well. Those you love and are sworn to protect are in danger of being treated as was my family. I am here to implore you to act now, while there is still time to thwart his desires. I would see no others suffer as I and my family have."

For a moment after she stopped speaking there was no sound at all in the room. Then a murmur rose from the men, mingling expressions of outrage, sympathy and determination starting low but rising to a near roar. Jeoffrey finally stood and held up both hands to request silence. After a moment the men complied.

Jeoffrey thanked her and suggested to the group they must consider how best to answer Sir William's attacks. Rosalind took that as her cue to leave the group. Tremors of relief shook her and her legs wobbled as she made her way from the room. Several of the gentlemen stood to kiss her hand or just express their regret for what she'd suffered. She thanked them and then rushed outside and stopped on the lawn, drawing in huge breaths of clean, fresh air, before she joined the throng of ladies.

Feeling in need of refreshment, Rosalind went first to the trestles set up along one side and got a cup of spiced apple juice blended with wine. It was tangy and bracing. She watched a group of women playing Pall Mall while she drank. The group laughed and chattered while making sporadic attempts to coax their balls through the colored wickets. A small group sat on a cloth spread on the ground, playing a card game.

Jane found her as she stood by the table.

"How went it?" she asked.

Rosalind shrugged. "I was able to convey my story to them, and there seemed to be much anger and outrage as a result. Whether that will translate into action is yet to be decided."

"We shall see." The woman gave her a sly smile. "If their answer is not what we believe it should be, we will know our work is not yet done."

"Truly," Rosalind sighed in agreement. She couldn't contemplate telling her story again with any comfort.

"For now, though, we must leave it in their hands. Come join us for a round of Pall Mall."

Rosalind joined their game with enthusiasm but little success in propelling her ball through the wickets. Though she did her best to keep her attention focused on the game and the ladies around her, it wandered often to thoughts of what transpired within the manor. Occasional raucous shouts floated out through doors left open to admit the warm, late-spring breeze. Sometimes the din expressed approval and agreement; at other times it held notes of conflict or anger.

By late afternoon, the ladies began to tire of their games and started to drift back inside to rest before dressing for dinner. Rosalind helped the servants clear the trestles and remove everything back inside before she went to dress.

She stopped outside the great hall and listened to the debate for a moment, but the men were discussing weaknesses in certain fortresses. It told her nothing about the tenor of the debate and whether it moved in the direction she felt necessary.

Glennys came quickly when Rosalind rang for her and helped her bathe and dress in the grandest of the clothes they'd borrowed from Jeoffrey's mother. A magnificent blue velvet houppeland trimmed in lighter blue satin, worn open at the front to display the pale blue, lace-edged smock beneath it. A chaperone of rolled blue satin with a veil that ended just above her eyes matched the fabric of the houppelande.

When she stood, Glennys clapped and sighed at the sight she made, so Rosalind presumed she carried the grand clothing well enough.

As she returned to front of the manor, meaning to skirt the great hall on her way to the kitchens, she met several of the men, making their way toward their quarters. All acknowledged her politely. Their expressions varied from an exuberant joy to grim sternness. She looked for Jeoffrey among them and finally found him just exiting the great hall.

"My lord," she said to him. Then, on catching a better look at his face, she added, "My lord, are you well?"

"My lady," he acknowledged. "Well enough. Just tired."

"You have some time to rest before dinner," Rosalind suggested.

"I will try to do so."

Rosalind paused, wondering if his reticence indicated a failure he hesitated to discuss. "Did your talks not go well?" she asked.

He pulled a small smile from the exhausted planes of his face. "Aye, they went to our purpose. We gather quickly, a fortnight from today, at Chilton, from whence we can proceed in a day's time to Railles. I am off to the king three days hence to inform him of our plans and reaffirm our loyalty."

"Though battle is never an end to be sought for its own sake," Rosalind said, "In this instance it appears our only hope for long survival, so I am grateful for your efforts, my lord. Now, please go rest."

"My thanks." He bowed and left her.

Rosalind proceeded to the kitchen to be sure all was in order there, then checked with the butler, majordomo and steward to ensure they were prepared as well. She found the musicians who'd play for dinner and dancing setting up their instruments in the minstrel's loft. They requested water be available and she went to obtain a pitcher and cups for them.

Dinner was an exuberant, boisterous affair. Though he looked only somewhat revived after a rest, Jeoffrey started it off with a short speech congratulating his guests on taking the decision to move now rather than wait for another disaster. There were numerous toasts by other lords and gentlemen to themselves, the families they strove to protect, the king, the land, and most of all to victory. Much laughter, joking, eating and drinking ensued.

Jane congratulated her on the success of her efforts, though Rosalind felt it owed more to Jeoffrey's leadership and the fear of Sir William's unbridled ambition. She began to feel a prickling of fear concerning the outcome of the battle.

"We have achieved one goal," she said to Jane. "Now, what can we do to aid them in finding victory in battle?"

"You have already done much," Jane answered. "In showing them what they can expect from defeat at Sir William's hands. For the rest..." She thought for a minute. "We can see they have adequate supplies, but truly there's little else we can do. All depends on the strength, courage and cleverness of our men. I trust they can do this. I also know that it will cost some their lives or dearly in wounds. I dread that," she admitted. "I dread it especially for James and these other men I know and respect."

"Still, we know 'tis the cost of what we seek to accomplish."

"Aye." Jane shook her head and drew out a smile. "But for this evening, we celebrate. Tomorrow we can begin to worry. For tonight we will banish gloomy forebodings and enjoy what we have. You are looking especially well this evening, Lady Rosalind. That houppeland becomes you well."

Rosalind returned the compliment and followed the other woman's lead in dispatching her darker fears to a deeper part of her heart. The meal repaid her efforts in preparation. Food came and went in abundance, haunches of meat were brought out and promptly carved down to bare bone, bowls of fruit disappeared, wine and ale flowed, a bard performed, then the tables were moved back to make room for dancing.

Rosalind had learned most common dance steps shortly after she learned to walk. It was one of her favorite activities and helped to banish her worries. When she partnered with Jeoffrey, she struggled to keep her yearning for him from showing on her face. She knew from his solemn glances tempered by the occasional wink or gleam he had the same difficulty.

Eventually the candles began to flicker and lords and ladies retired from the room. The musicians finished their last set and sought well-earned refreshment. The servants cleared the last of the cups and trenchers from the room. Rosalind retired last of all, bidding goodnight to Jeoffrey and a few of the other men who remained in the room for a last consultation. Glennys helped her out of the elaborate clothes and into a plain nightshirt, then the girl departed.

She expected sleep to come quickly after the exhaustions of the day, but it didn't. She felt she waited for something and didn't know what it was until the soft knock roused her from the bed. She got up and welcomed Jeoffrey into the room. They barely remembered to shut the door behind them before they crashed together, body to body, mouth to mouth.

They made love, hot, hard and quick, stripping clothes off as they kissed their way across the room, barely making it to the bed before he plunged into her. Few words passed between them, but many inchoate sounds of tension and pleasure, and it didn't take long before the spasms of completion engulfed them both. When they could move enough to draw apart, Jeoffrey rolled off her and to her side, settling her against him, wrapped in his arms.

"I needed that," he said. "After only a night, I miss you in my bed more than I can say. And not just your body. Last night I longed for your company, to talk to you about…"

He appeared unwilling to complete the sentence. "About what, Jeoffrey?" she prompted, "Our coming unions with others?"

"Nay, not that," he said, "though there is some discussion needed on that as well."

"Then what?" she asked.

He didn't answer. The light in the room was too dim to let her see much of his expression, but she felt him grow tense.

"Jeoffrey? Is something wrong?"

"I know not whether 'tis wrong," he said. The words sounded difficult—as though he forced them out. "But 'tis shaming. And you are the only person in the world to whom I can imagine admitting it."

"What?"

"I'm worried," he said. "Possibly even fearful."

Chapter Sixteen

Rosalind considered her response carefully. "I cannot imagine you being afraid of anything, Jeoffrey. You are the bravest man I know. When you rescued me…you took a huge risk that night, and you did not seem overly concerned about it. What do you fear? Battle? Defeat? Being injured…or worse?"

"Nay," he said. "None of those, or…those only in some degree. I will not consider the possibility of defeat. And I respect the dangers of battle and the possibility of injury or death. Those are the risks a knight takes. They concern me, but not so much as…"

She waited for him to continue.

"I have never led an army before," he said. "At most I have led a company of men I know and who know me. I understand how to manage a small group for best effect in someone else's larger plan."

He drew a long, hard breath. "I have been anointed leader of this attack," he said. "I truly know not if I am worthy of that. I know not that I can bring them into the jaws of death and send some to the next life. And how can I feel confident the battle plan I have created will give us the best chance of victory or that I can lead them with enough determination and authority to gain their greatest efforts?" His voice shook as he said, "I fear I shall fail them. And with them, all who depend on those brave knights. 'Tis a daunting thing to have so much responsibility in one's own inadequate hands."

"Aye, that it is." Rosalind thought about his doubts and how to respond to them. "Were all in agreement concerning the course of action to take against Sir William?" she asked him.

She felt him relax at the question. "Nay, of course not. Some thought we should seek the king's intervention, some were for battle but not just yet, a few wanted to hold parlay with William to arrange a truce. Fools."

"Did all finally come around to your point of view?"

"Most, not all."

"And how did you bring them to your side?"

He stopped for a moment of recall. "In truth, I know not, exactly. I reviewed the situation with them, gave my views, told what I thought needed to be done, then listened to their objections and answered them as best I could. I had support and help from those who shared my view from the start. Some I had to approach privately, to answer their fears and hesitations directly. Others had to be convinced Sir William's defeat could be accomplished."

"And you were able to convince them."

"Aye."

"Think you 'tis more difficult to direct the hearts and actions of men in council or on the battlefield?"

"In council, of course. Well-trained knights know what to do on the battlefield and respond to the orders of their commander."

"Yet, this thing you have just done. And how did you go about laying your plans for battle?"

"We considered what must be done and ways it might be achieved. I laid out my ideas, others offered theirs, they agreed my idea seemed most likely to succeed but offered suggestions for improvements. Many of those were adopted."

"I see. Jeoffrey, I understand your worries. Sometimes circumstances be not what they appear or luck goes against one and you lose despite your best efforts. There is no way to protect against those things. It appears to me you and the others have done all in your power to lay a plan with the best chance of success. And in choosing you to lead this group, I truly believe they also made a move they felt gained them the best person to take charge of it. If you continue to deny your fitness for this post, you also demean the judgment of all here. Can you truly say so many are all guilty of such poor discernment?"

After a long moment when he was very still and silent, he said, "Nay, I dare not." He relaxed somewhat and even laughed softly. "Rosalind." He breathed her name on a soft sigh, pulled her hard against him and bound her in his arms so tightly she knew he hated to let her go. "You cannot imagine how much I want to throw over all duty and obligation, just to keep you ever at my side."

"I can well imagine it. I feel much the same way. Yet in my case, I have no say in the decision."

"Not so," he said, and he suddenly put her far enough away to let her see his face. Moonlight streamed in the window to illuminate the sparks in his gray eyes. He supported himself on his elbows, but one hand stroked her cheek. "Rosalind, do you ask me right now to put aside my lordship and my obligations, for your sake, I will do so."

Shocked into stillness herself and moved almost to tears by the sudden offer, heart aching as she absorbed the enormity of what he'd just tendered, she reached out to touch him. She ran her hand down along his lean cheek, over the angle of his jaw, then up again over his ear, feeling the fine, soft strands of his blond hair. She was so tempted to take him at his word, to make the request, to bind him to her so she'd never have to let him go.

She'd never wanted anything so much in her life, and he was offering it to her freely. In the few short weeks she'd known him, he'd come to mean everything to her. He was her world: her joy, her protector, her lord and master, her lover, her friend. She couldn't imagine another man for whom she could have such feelings. None other could be so brave and strong, yet so gentle at the same time, so kind and yet so firm. No other man would play silly word games with her, discipline her so lovingly, love her so sweetly or understand so thoroughly her fears and needs. A future without him loomed bleak, joyless and achingly empty.

If she accepted the offer he made from the depths of his gratitude and love, he would do as he promised, abandon his beliefs about what he owed others and give all to her. His honor would insist he keep the promise and he would do so.

And it would break him.

To abandon the path honor had set him on, he would have to cut out large pieces of his soul, his pride, his loyalty, his sense of integrity, everything that made him the man he was. He would do it, but the cost would be immeasurable. The man she would get would not be the man she'd come to love.

"Nay, Jeoffrey. Much though I am tempted to accept your offer, I cannot. We are who we are, and our true love for each other is based on that. Should I ask this of you, we would both become other people, and I think we would eventually find we neither of us liked those people. We will go on as honor and duty demand."

He sighed and held her tightly for a few minutes, his body stiff and tense, then he relaxed and said, "There are so many things I will miss about you, Rosalind. Not least of them is your remarkable wisdom for one so young. I know not how I can live without you."

"Nor do I contemplate a future without you with any pleasure, my lord. But life continues, and we, at least, have the gift of knowing our love exists even if we cannot share it together."

"Aye," he said, low, almost painfully. "Tomorrow we must talk of plans for the future. For tonight, however, I should be returning to my quarters."

In fact, though, it was quite a bit later before he finally extracted himself from her bed and made his way to the door.

They had no chance to talk until after the midday meal the next day, since the morning saw the departure of most of their guests. Aside from bidding them a courteous Godspeed, Jeoffrey had many things that required second consultations and confirmations with the various men.

By midday, only the duke remained. He ate an informal repast with them and then retired to his quarters to rest. His wife and daughter were expected to arrive later that afternoon.

Once he'd departed, Jeoffrey and Rosalind went to the office. He kissed and held her for a few moments before letting her go and backing away.

Without preamble, Jeoffrey said, "I have had several tentative offers for your hand. I hope one of them will prove agreeable to you."

"From whom, my lord?"

"Some from lords I would warn you not to consider," he answered. "Sir Bartram de Colray queried me about you, but I warned him off. He's handsome and well-settled, but he has a bad reputation. I would not be easy in mind were you with him. Sir Arnor expressed strong interest, but he is a third son and his means are questionable."

"According to Jane, Lady Shelton, rather, he is also somewhat simple."

"Aye, but of good heart. You could do worse."

"True."

"Andrew of Conneth also offered. His means are modest but not uncomfortable and he is a man of honor. Though older, he's reputed to be kind. And Sir Michel inquired as well, though he is quite old and frail."

"Lady Shelton mentioned him as well. She thinks he would be a fine match for me."

"Sir Michel? How so?"

"I would likely find myself a rich widow in fairly short order."

He looked shocked. "I had no idea Lady Shelton was so hard of heart."

"Nay, not hard of heart, my lord. Realistic. We ladies have so few choices available to us, and so much rides on them, including our very survival, we must be very careful about how we make them. A close, unflinching look at every side of an issue is necessary. We learn quickly to make the best of what choices we have."

"And truly," she continued, "does an old man make an offer for a young woman without understanding that while he expects to gain an ornament and perhaps a comfort for his last years, she expects to gain some wealth in return?"

"Your point is well made," he conceded. "As usual."

"Thank you, my lord. Are those my choices?"

"There is one other." He hesitated as though he didn't want to voice this one. "Sir Philip has also requested he be considered a candidate. His means are slim right now, but should we win this battle, his reward will be considerable. Even should we lose, his father is well off and his wife or widow would not go wanting."

She took a minute to consider those candidates. Though a couple of suits could be easily dismissed, there were still two she would entertain, though each led to a considerably different future.

"Must I give you a decision right now, my lord? I cannot but feel the outcome of your battle will have a grave influence on all of us and might change some circumstances greatly."

"I warned all inquirers we would take time to consider the many suits for you. But, Rosalind, please, do not count too much on what the changed circumstances past the battle might bring."

She recognized the emotions that underlay his warning. "Whatever hopes I entertain, my lord, will, of necessity, be subservient to what is realistic and proper."

He nodded slowly and looked pained.

Following up on the thought, she said, "May I ask if you have had any talk with the duke concerning the hopes you entertain?"

He sighed and nodded slowly. "We have discussed a possible alliance between our families."

"So he will be committing his resources to the effort against Sir William?"

"He will."

"I understand," Rosalind said, feeling her stomach clench and her mood darken. She'd anticipated it would play out so, had known this was the end they'd come to. But she hadn't wanted to believe it, had tried to deny to herself the inevitability of his betrothal to the Lady Alys, even while knowing all the time it was the course his honor and his concern for the people in his care demanded. And now more so than ever if the duke's aid rested on Jeoffrey's acceding to the Lady Alys' desire for a match with him. Rosalind's hope had remained alive on the expectation things might be otherwise, but it now had to fade and die.

"Thank you, my lord. I will consider which suit seems most… agreeable. For the nonce, though, I must make sure all is in readiness for the duchess and Lady Alys."

She'd thought the duke had traveled in great state with his many escorts and carts, but the entourage accompanying the Duchess of Barnston made his arrival seem commonplace. The grand carriage with the ducal crest was preceded by two carts of supplies, a troop of two dozen knights, two smaller carriages crammed with maids, while a miniature carriage for the duchess's lapdog and a small army of footmen and other servants trailed behind. The parade stretched so far it took almost thirty minutes for all to make their way into the manor courtyard to be emptied and dispersed.

Lady Alys alighted first from the carriage, looking around with critical eyes until she spotted Jeoffrey awaiting her. Her face broke into a huge, possessive smile, and she ran to him, ignoring propriety, to stop before him. "My lord, Jeoffrey," she said offering a hand and waiting for him to kiss it as courtesy demanded. He did so, graciously, but with perhaps a slight reluctance the others might not even have noticed.

Lady Alys was a tall young woman with dark hair and fine dark eyes. Slender build, strong, regular teeth and a shapely nose combined to make her attractive though not beautiful or even pretty. Her bearing was at once stately and haughty, showing the confidence of one used to getting whatever she wanted. And right now she made it clear to all she very much wanted Jeoffrey.

The duchess stood beside the carriage watching her daughter's actions and making no attempt to hide her disapproval. In fact, it appeared, as she swept her gaze across the manor, the grounds and the people waiting to greet her, everything she saw failed her standards. Unlike her daughter, the duchess had once been a beauty. She remained a strikingly handsome woman, though lines around her eyes and at the corner of a perpetually frowning mouth had blurred the beautiful lines of her face.

Her husband came forward to greet her and accompany her to make her courtesy to Jeoffrey, though they had to move their daughter aside to do so. They then proceeded to acknowledge Rosalind.

The duke introduced her as the Earl of Highwaith's daughter, who'd been rescued by Lord Jeoffrey and remained under his protection pending arrangements for her future. Rosalind could see the duchess jump immediately to impolite but correct conclusions.

Rosalind curtseyed and said, "Your grace, welcome to Blaisdell. I hope you will find all arranged for you comfort during your stay."

The duchess sniffed. "I expect it to be." She proceeded into the house with no further word.

Smarting from the snub but trying not to let it affect her, Rosalind turned and followed the rest of the group into the manor. When they stopped in the great hall, she rang for a servant to bring refreshements, but the duchess overruled her by saying, "I would like to go straight to our quarters to freshen up. The journey was not pleasant and I am much in need of restoring. Show us to them immediately, *Lady* Rosalind, and have a measure of spiced cider and cooled water sent there right away as well."

Rosalind stiffened her spine, gave herself a stern lecture about keeping her temper in check, and led the duchess and her daughter to their quarters. She wasn't surprised when the two women agreed their chambers were rather smaller than they might have expected, the furnishings not grand enough and the air held a slightly disagreeable aroma.

"And there is no fire in the grate." The duchess turned to Rosalind. "I'm surprised, my lady, that such a thing could have been overlooked."

"The weather has been so fine, no one else wished for one, your grace," she said. "But of course, I will have one laid for you immediately."

"Indeed. Are you sure this room was properly aired?"

"It was, your grace. I saw to it myself."

"Hmmm," the duchess intoned, implying volumes about Rosalind's competence.

"If your grace would prefer other quarters I am sure we can arrange something."

"Are these the best chambers you have?"

"Saving his lordship's private chambers, they are.

"And what would you know of his lordship's private chambers?" the duchess accused. "Surely even you have enough sense of decorum to know that a gentleman's chambers should be off limits to any lady save his wife."

"Of course, in general circumstances, it's true, but there are occasions when my service to his lordship demands I enter his quarters to retrieve something for him or bring something he wishes."

The duchess sniffed again and remarked on how poor their servants were if a *lady* performed such errands.

The servants arrived with the drinks the duchess had requested. She naturally found fault with those too, but conceded with ill grace she'd accept them to avoid creating additional work. Rosalind was very careful to be sure her thanks held no shred of sarcasm.

Rosalind was eventually able to retreat, leaving them to refresh themselves and rest from their journey. She heaved a huge sigh of relief to be away and wondered how she could possibly survive two more days of their biting words and haughty snubs. She'd have to, however, and bear it with good grace, for Jeoffrey's sake. Much, possibly his entire future, rested on their approval of him. Fortunately it didn't rest on their approval of her, or there would be no hope at all, she thought, allowing herself a bit of humor to wash away the bad odor they left lingering in her nostrils.

Dinner was an enormous challenge. Though her seating plan had called for the duke to be placed at Jeoffrey's immediate right with his daughter beyond and then the duchess and herself, Rosalind noted that Lady Alys took it upon herself to switch her place with the duke's so that she sat on Jeoffrey's right. The duchess noticed and frowned over it, but said nothing. About that, at least. She had a great deal to say about other things: the food, the drink, the service, the surroundings, the accommodations, and the company. None of it was positive.

Rosalind struggled through dinner, answering calmly when she could and feigning difficulty hearing when she despaired of maintaining her composure should she speak.

Lady Alys ate little but drank more wine than was wise. She spoke too much, laughed too loudly, and flirted shamefully with Jeoffrey. The duchess looked her way several times, her eyes angry, and once she leaned over and murmured something to her husband. Her glance at her daughter suggested she wanted him to try to restrain the girl. The duke shrugged and leaned over toward Lady Alys.

The young woman huffed and looked irritated when her father voiced his displeasure with her behavior. She shook her head and argued, then finally sniffed again and turned back to Jeoffrey. Gentle as her own parents had been with her, Rosalind would never have dared defy their wishes so openly.

She held her peace through dinner and the entertainment afterwards, though the duchess's constant harping and Lady Alys's audacious flirting combined to wear on her nerves. By the time she was able to crawl into bed, the effort of keeping a rein on her temper had exhausted her. She knew Jeoffrey wouldn't be there that night, and she missed him, but only briefly before she fell into a shallow sleep interrupted several times by bad dreams.

She woke with a foreboding she hoped meant nothing more than a long day made difficult by a poor night's sleep and the daunting prospect of entertaining the duchess and her daughter all day.

It wasn't to be so easy, however.

Rosalind kept her calm until midday when the duchess's criticisms grew even more frequent and intense after a morning walk to the river and then a lunch that was neither abundant enough, nor grand enough for her.

After a while, Rosalind was able to separate out enough of her mind to recognize that much of the criticism grew out of the duchess's disapproval of the match with Jeoffrey, and was an attempt on her part to convince her daughter the place wasn't suitable for her. In that it failed utterly. Lady Alys was far too besotted with Jeoffrey to concern herself with whether the food or the quarters met some highly exacting standard.

Her failure did nothing to improve the duchess's humor or to sway her from the course she'd chosen.

But it wore on Rosalind's temper like a tab of rough, stiff cloth rubbing the skin until it started to wear away, leaving a bleeding wound that grew worse each time the tab touched it.

If she could have found any decent excuse to stay away from dinner, she would have. But as Jeoffrey's hostess, duty demanded she be present, and even the entirely real headache she had didn't provide sufficient justification for failing that obligation.

The duchess had expanded her list of complaints to include the servants, who didn't always respond quickly enough, and Jeoffrey himself for allowing such lax attention from his staff.

Rosalind tried to explain the servants had been working around the clock for nearly a week and they were trying to give them all some time off by rotating who was on duty. It left them a little short, but not unbearably so. While the duchess brushed off her explanation with a sweeping gesture and "Servants should only be allowed time off when 'tis convenient for their betters," Rosalind watched Lady Alys fawning over Jeoffrey.

She had watched Jeoffrey persuade the duke to sit next to him that night, then they both had to hide grimaces of annoyance when Lady Alys pretended to have lost her handkerchief and switched chairs while her father gallantly sought the missing cloth. Lady Alys had flirted openly with Jeoffrey since the beginning of the meal, but her advances were becoming cruder and more blatant. She found excuses to touch him, wiping a pretend crumb from his lips and brushing hair from his face.

Jeoffrey was just removing the young lady's hand from his thigh when her mother stated, "This is just intolerable. My cup has been empty for a minute or more and no one has come to refill it. Does Lord Jeoffrey make any attempt to keep proper discipline among his servants?"

The comment caught Rosalind already fuming about Lady Alys's advances. It made her furious on behalf of her lord and his staff. With the exhaustion accumulated from the previous days weakening her, Rosalind lost her hold on her temper. She stood, picked up the pitcher nearby, and filled the duchess's cup, barely restraining herself from bashing it over the woman's head, but she could hold her tongue no longer.

"God's blood, Madame! You proclaim our household discipline inferior because a servant does not come the very second of your desire to do something you could perfectly well do for yourself, while at the same time your shameless hussy of a daughter makes the most disgustingly forward advances on my lord. How dare you complain about discipline in this household when you fail to enforce proper behavior on your own daughter?"

As the room when silent around her, Rosalind realized what a devastating error she'd made.

Chapter Seventeen

All eyes in the room focused on her. Rosalind froze for a minute, shocked by her own words. When it wore off she hoped a lightning bolt would come and strike her down or the Judgment Day trumpet would choose that moment to sound.

Neither happened and Rosalind had to face the fact she'd just done the unforgivable.

The duchess stared at her, eyes wide and furious, mouth agape, for a moment, then she drew a very long breath and said, "Well, I never... This is completely outrageous. Your behavior, young lady, is quite beyond the pale. You dare accuse me of allowing my daughter to behave badly, yet she would never accost a guest in such a rude, insulting, infamous way."

Rosalind stood there groping for something to say or do to mitigate the effects of her behavior. The duchess's words made clear how she'd shamed not just herself, but Jeoffrey as well. She turned to him and saw him watching her with shocked horror. She couldn't meet his gaze.

She had to apologize, to say something to put things right. If it could be done at all.

"Your grace, you are entirely correct," she said, turning to the woman, and forcing the words past the huge obstruction in her throat. "My words were disgraceful and infamous and I very much regret them. I offer my most sincere and abject apologies."

She turned to Jeoffrey again. "And to you, as well, my lord. I regret the shame I have brought on your household with my disgraceful behavior."

And then, watching him, she knew what she had to do, though she dreaded it with every fiber of her being. "My lord, I request that I be disciplined for this shocking display of poor behavior."

She did meet his gaze this time, and tried to read the frown on his face as a gauge to how angry he was with her.

"You will get down on your knees right here and apologize to each person. Then I think it best you leave us," he said.

Rosalind started to breathe a sigh of relief, until the duchess said, "Really, Lord Jeoffrey, think you 'tis sufficient? Behavior such as this would not be tolerated in my household and would be answered with a severe punishment. I had heard you attempted to run a well-ordered household with stern discipline."

They both looked at Jeoffrey. Rosalind doubted any of the others understood the depth of his conflict, and she hated herself for putting him in this untenable position.

"My lord," she said, holding his eyes, "I realize that with guests present you might believe it wiser to conduct your discipline in private, yet I feel such unbearable shame and remorse, I would have it expiated here and now. I beg you to proceed as would be normal, regarding our guests in the nature of family for this purpose."

His hard, solemn expression didn't change as he watched her for a long, silent, nearly unbearable moment while he considered her request. No one else could have read it, but she saw in his eyes the plea for her to release them both from the unbearable situation and take the outlet he'd offered. She held his gaze and refused to relent.

Finally he nodded. "So be it." He turned to a servant who'd frozen in place nearby when the crisis began and said, "Fetch Joseph and Wulfram and tell them to bring in the punishment bench, then find Master Chrestien and ask him to come and bring the straight rod with him."

The boy nodded and left the room.

For a moment the stillness was so profound when one man coughed it echoed through the room like the report of an explosion.

Jeoffrey said, "We will still have that apology, Lady Rosalind. On your knees."

The ground grew shaky beneath her as she dropped carefully to her knees, adjusting the skirts of her houppeland. A tear broke loose and ran down her cheek, leaving a hot wet streak. The air around her seemed to thicken, grow gray and misty. She murmured another apology, heartfelt and abject, though she would have no idea later what she said, and tried to keep from falling over. Her body trembled so hard she was unsure of her balance.

Behind her she heard the scrape and clatter as the bench was placed in position. She looked up when the groom walked up next to her to await his lord's orders. She couldn't help but glance at the object he carried. A straight rod it was, a fearsome length of supple wood, nearly a yard long and perhaps half an inch in diameter.

"What is your will, my lord?" the groom asked.

Jeoffrey nodded to her. "Lady Rosalind has committed a grave lapse in judgment and demeanor. She has been intolerably insulting to a guest. You will put her on the bench, as is, and administer a dozen cuts with the rod."

The groom sucked in a hard, sharp breath. "Aye, my lord," he acknowledged, though she could hear the shock and dismay in his voice. The man turned to her. "Lady Rosalind?" He offered a hand to help her to her feet and she accepted the help gratefully. Blinded by the tears now flooding her eyes, shaking so hard she could barely move on her own, she doubted she could make it even the few steps to the bench without assistance. Terror stole most of her breath. She'd thought he'd order two or three strokes, enough to let her know she'd been punished, enough to be humiliating, not so much as to cause serious pain.

"Face down on the bench, please, my lady," the groom requested. "Wulfram take her hands, Thomas her feet."

She felt each of the young men holding her in place and waited for the groom to flip her skirts up. He didn't and there was a tiny relief in that.

All relief died as she heard the whistling sound of the rod cutting through the air and the smack as it met her flesh. The pain followed right behind the noise, a dense, burning sensation across her derriere. It wasn't nearly as vicious as it would have been had not several layers of clothes cushioned the impact, but it still smarted. She drew a sharp breath and clamped her lips shut. She would not give anyone the satisfaction of hearing her cry out.

The rod struck again, a little lower, and she flinched as it spread an aching fire in her flesh. The young man stationed at her head held her wrists firmly, preventing her from doing more than wiggling a bit, but not hard enough to bruise or hurt her. She opened her eyes, but her arm blocked her view of the room. It would also keep anyone from seeing her face as she accepted the pain.

She turned her face to the other side and looked up over her arm. The groom stood above her on this side. The rod rose again and flicked down. Pain slashed through her but she kept still and silent while she fought to absorb it. The groom was striking hard, but the clothes protected her from the worst of it. "As is" Jeoffrey had said, and she understood his calculation that the punishment would look more severe than it truly was.

Which didn't mean it was fun or easy. Her tormentor worked the cuts from the middle of her bottom down along the tops of her thighs and then back up again. None of the strokes were particularly harder or gentler than all the others, though as it went on, the cumulative burn, when he struck over flesh already flaming, was enough to make her hiss through her teeth and try to wriggle away from it.

By the end, she was so dizzy and numb from the effects of emotion too mixed and forceful to hold easily, she barely registered the last couple of strokes. She almost hated when it was over and the two young men released her. She would now have to stand and face the witnesses to her humiliation. The groom helped her to her feet and spoke very quietly. "I regret having to cause you this pain, my lady," he whispered almost in her ear. "We respect what you did."

"You did your duty and did it quite perfectly as always, Master Chrestien," she answered, just as softly. "I hold nothing against you. In truth, I am quite grateful."

She straightened herself and turned to meet Jeoffrey's eyes. She couldn't bear to look at any of the others and didn't. She detected a hint of anguish and compassion in his stern expression, but none of that was in his voice when he said, "Thank you, Master Chrestien. Lady Rosalind, you are dismissed to your quarters, where you will remain until this time tomorrow, on bread and water, meditating on your poor behavior, and, I trust, resolving to do better in the future."

"Yes, my lord."

Fortunately, she could exit the room without having to face the duchess or Lady Alys again. Rosalind attempted to make her exit as graceful and dignified as possible. The physical pain had already faded almost to nothing, but her face still flamed with the emotional anguish. She was so lost in the humiliation and fear of what her behavior might have done, she was halfway to her quarters before she realized the gift Jeoffrey had given her. By confining her to quarters for the next twenty-four hours, he spared her the necessity of having to see or deal with the duke, duchess, or Lady Alys again. They were scheduled to depart in the morning.

Once in her solar she curled up on the bed and finally let flow the tears she'd been holding back for what seemed like hours. She had cried herself into a half-doze when a soft, tentative knock sounded at the door and Glennys entered.

"My lady? How do you?" the girl asked. She saw Rosalind on the bed and came over. "Need you a poultice or some ointment?"

"Nay. I am not in that kind of pain."

"My lady..." Glennys stopped and swallowed. "My lady, I wanted to say I admire how very brave you were to speak up to that... to the duchess just so, and to defend our lord and the household. All the staff... Well, we do know what you did on our behalf, and we appreciate it. And then you were even braver to let him punish you so he would not look bad before them. You are much more truly a lady than some that have higher titles."

"Glennys, I... I thank you heartily," Rosalind said, surprised and moved by the girl's understanding and gratitude.

"Are you sure there is naught you need?" Glennys asked.

"Nay. My lord was careful to organize my discipline so it would look and sound far worse than it was. In truth, there is no soreness remaining at all."

She let Glennys help her out of the lovely houppeland and fancy shift and into a plain smock with her warm robe over it. Once she was comfortable, she dismissed the girl, saying she planned to go quickly to sleep.

She had climbed into bed, but wasn't yet asleep when another knock sounded. The door opened carefully and Elspeth stuck her head in. "My lady?" she called so softly it wouldn't have roused her had she been asleep.

"I am awake," Rosalind said. "Come in. Have you a candle?"

"Aye, my lady." She went back to the hall and brought it in to light the room. "I regret to disturb your ladyship, but there is something I must needs do." Rosalind nodded for her to go on, but for a moment the housekeeper couldn't seem to find the words.

"My lady, I just wanted to say, on behalf of all the staff, that we regret you had to suffer as you did this evening, but we are very grateful to you for defending us. Though it was not, perhaps, terribly wise of you, it was gallant. I truly hope you do not find yourself in much distress, and if so, I would see what we might find for your relief."

The tears threatened again as she listened to the housekeeper's praise and concern. She remembered how slow this woman had been to accept her presence and position in the household. This was more than she could have ever wished.

"Truly, Elspeth, I am in no discomfort. In body, anyway. My lord was careful to ensure the punishment would seem harsh but cause little pain," she repeated.

"Of course," Elspeth said. "'Tis harder to accept the humbling nature of it. And to know that despic... the duchess and the others were enjoying it at your expense."

Rosalind couldn't hold onto the tears as the housekeeper put her pain into words. "Aye," she admitted.

Elspeth squeezed her lips together and her eyes narrowed. She hesitated, drawing a quick breath, then she came and sat beside Rosalind on the bed, put her arms around the younger woman and drew her head against her shoulder. Rosalind was both shocked and comforted by the gesture, which reminded her of something her mother might have done in similar circumstances. She leaned into the woman, and let her tears flow.

"It was even worse," she said, between sobs, "because I knew I had embarrassed and humiliated Lord Jeoffrey. He put so much trust in me, having me act as his hostess, and I disappointed him. And then I put him in the awful position of having to choose between not correcting me and thus proving the duchess' accusations about the discipline in his house or ordering his hostess to be punished in the presence of his guests." She wept hard, soaking the shoulder of the woman's dress. "He must be very angry and disappointed with me."

Elspeth stroked her back gently and brushed hair away from her face. "Nay, my lady, I doubt he is angry with you."

"He must be."

"Nay. Master Chrestien sought him out after dinner. He was not happy about what Lord Jeoffrey asked him to do to you. My lord explained the situation and how you both sought to find the best solution to a serious error. But my lord also said he was not surprised you had finally been overcome and unable to control yourself any longer. He was amazed you held on as long as you had. He just regretted your lapse was so loud and public. In fact, I think my lord blames himself somewhat for putting you in the position of having to take so much of that harrid — the duchess' complaints."

"She will not be a comfortable mother-in-law for him."

Elspeth sighed long and deep. "Nay. Nor comfortable for us to have visiting. We all do as we must, however."

"Aye." Rosalind sniffed and sighed deeply.

Elspeth handed her a cloth and stood up. "My lady, if you are sure there is naught else you need, I have work to do yet. I will bid you goodnight."

"Thank you, Elspeth, you have given me the best medicine possible for my pain."

Calmed and comforted, she settled into bed and quickly fell asleep this time. If anyone else came to the door, she failed to notice or rouse.

Rosalind actually enjoyed the unaccustomed luxury of remaining in bed in the morning even after sunlight began to stream through her window. She rose only when a sharp knock preceded the entrance of Glennys to help her dress.

"I will fetch your breakfast now, my lady," she said afterward. "Would you have an egg or jam? We believe my lord's restrictions on food were more to confirm his confining you here as a punishment than because he truly meant to short you."

"Nay," Rosalind answered. "Bread and water were ordered; bread and water it shall be. In truth…" She laughed a little. "I have had too much rich food and drink the past few days. The prospect of plain bread and water, eaten peacefully in isolation, appeals greatly."

Glennys smiled back at her and nodded.

Had her thoughts not been so preoccupied by speculations on the future and on how Jeoffrey felt about her faux pas, she would have enjoyed the peace and tranquility of a day when she had no calls on her time and no one to entertain or plan for. Glennys collected embroidery materials for her and Rosalind began a project, reacquainting herself with the soothing effect of stitching and the pleasure in watching beautiful patterns emerge.

The day slid by easily until the light began to dim at the window. Rosalind wondered when she should be released from her confinement. Bread and water had sufficed for most of the day, but now her stomach rumbled with the desire for more substantial fare.

She was about to release herself and go in search of a snack, but before she could do so, the door opened and Jeoffrey himself marched into the room.

"Lady Rosalind," he said. "You appear well-rested. Are you well?"

"Well enough, my lord," she answered, trying to gauge his mood. His expression was stern, set in hard lines, though not openly angry. His tone was neutral.

"And you have no ill effects from your discipline yesterday?"

"None whatsoever, my lord. You were careful that would be so."

"Good," he said. "Then there will be no impediment to my taking you over my knee and giving you the spanking you truly deserve."

Chapter Eighteen

"Deserve?" Shock had driven her voice away so she could barely get the word out. "How so, my lord? Was I not sufficiently punished yesterday?"

"That discipline was for your insult to the duchess. This is for taking it upon yourself to force me into ordering the punishment, an act that outraged most of the household, by the way, and for leaving me, as a result, to cope with that entire family for the rest of the evening and this morning."

"Was it so difficult as that, my lord?" she asked.

"Worse." He sat on the side of her bed. "As you well know. Take off your clothes and come over here."

Still unsure of his mood, she removed her overrobe and shift, then stood nude before him. He took her arm and gently pulled her to him, flipped her over, and draped her across his knee. He slid back far enough on the bed she actually rested on it as well, with only her midsection raised over his lap.

He immediately began slapping her bottom with his hand, not terribly hard, but repeatedly and continuously. He worked up and down, from waist to thighs, going over and over it, until she knew the skin must be very red indeed and it was stinging quite sharply. She considered protesting and swallowed it. They had both been through a difficult, emotional event, and she'd made his situation much worse with her failure. Her discipline yesterday might have satisfied the duchess, but he knew well enough it had hurt her pride far worse than her body. Perhaps they both needed this to release their emotions over it.

It hurt, but it wasn't the same kind of pain she'd known yesterday. This stung more on her rear, but rather than grating her pride, it set alight something else in her body, rousing her longing for him. It was a sweet, fiery pain that made her ache in deep, womanly ways. She was sure he knew it, too, for he occasionally halted and explored her flesh, rubbing her derriere and tracing a curious finger down the crack to the private areas. When he rubbed at her slit, she could tell it was slick with the moisture of her desire for him. But then he would resume spanking her.

Even when she began to moan, he whaled away, ignoring her sobs and squeals, until she could bear it no longer and begged, "Please, my lord, can you forgive me yet? I apologize abjectly for all the wrongs I have done you the past few days, but I truly do not know that I can bear more punishment."

He deposited five more hard slaps on her bottom, making her screech and try to wiggle away, then he stopped, put one hand under her waist, the other below her knees, and flipped her over. He raised her head and wiped away the tears with his thumbs before he kissed her. His tongue did a slow, thorough exploration of her lips, then pushed through them to rub along her teeth and do a sinuous mating dance with her tongue. Her bottom throbbed—her entire body throbbed with need for him.

His hands moved over her, cupping her breasts, touching delicately at the sensitive tips, tracing around them, then over them, squeezing exquisitely until she was moaning aloud.

He tipped her back onto the bed and lay alongside her. His mouth went where his hands had lately explored, sucking and nibbling until she was writhing with pleasurable tension.

A trail of kisses down her belly to the joint of her legs made her groan again, wanting him, needing him. His hair skimmed her flesh along with his tongue, and its delicate brush contrasted sweetly with the rougher rasp.

His big, hard hands rubbed along her thighs, running down the front, coming up along the middle, brushing slowly, slowly higher until she ached to have his touch on the center of her need.

He parted the outer lips and explored within, first with gentle fingers, then with his mouth. Each stroke there sent flashes of lightning and white heat through her, winding her tighter, taking her higher. Yet just as she reached the point where she knew another lick would push her over the edge, he stopped and waited until she cooled a little. Then he went back to work, driving her to new heights of tension, stopped and waited once again.

After the second pause, when his tongue touched her again, it sent her into near-madness, and the explosion that followed had her body arching up off the bed, throbbing with relentless spasms of sheer ecstasy. He lay beside her and held her until the climax finally wore itself out and let her return to herself.

He brushed hair back from her face and leaned over to kiss her again. He started to move over her and she put a hand on his chest to hold him in place next to her. "Not yet, my lord," she whispered to him. "I have a favor to return to you."

She saw the puzzlement in his eyes turn to comprehension and delight as she leaned over him and loosened the laces of his tunic and shirt. She slid them over his head, and began to lick his chest, running her tongue up and down, tangling in the pale blond hair there, circling his flat nipples, and flicking over them until he groaned and reached for her.

She eluded his grasp by ducking lower. She skimmed her mouth down his chest to his abdomen, pushing his leggings down, skirting the hot, throbbing length of his cock, until she reached the joint where hip met thigh. After a brief pause while she removed his boots and hose, she trailed a hand down the front of one thigh, her lips down the other, then nudged his legs apart and slipped both hand and mouth around to the inside. They traveled up again, slowly, pinching lightly, licking and nipping. She reached the top. Faced with the hair-roughened balls, she hesitated a moment, looking up along his length to his face. He lay very still, only his chest rising and falling in fast rhythm. His eyes were closed tight and lips pinched together.

She reached out and cupped the heavy balls in her hand, playing her fingers over them, exploring this mystery that was exclusive to men. They felt surprisingly delicate in her hold. He let out a long, gasping moan. She reached higher, moving a tentative finger onto the base of his rod, starting to trace its length. The skin was soft but stretched tightly over hardness beneath. He groaned loudly and began to writhe just as she had before. She reached a spot just below the tip and rubbed gently at the slight ridge there.

The bed shook as he convulsed with pleasure. He moaned in an agony of near-unbearable pleasure. She moved her fingers onto the head of his cock, surprised by the contrast. It was softer and sleeker with a drop of fluid leaking from the end. His breath was coming in harsh gasps now.

Following his example, she leaned over and let her tongue trace the line up his shaft her finger had lately taken. He tasted a little salty, but she delighted in the power she had to give him pleasure beyond words. His body shook so hard, the bed posts groaned along with him. Her tongue reached the top and circled the bulb.

He suddenly arched and reached down to take her arms, pulled her up on top of him, then rolled over so he was above. He nudged her legs apart and found her entrance. They both grunted as his invasion stirred the dormant ache of tension into new life in her. He pushed in part of the way, several times, withdrew, and then finally plunged all the way in, burying himself inside. His balls slapped against her.

He tried to set a slow rhythm, to make it last longer, but their need was too great, and soon they came together in shattering, pulsing waves, their bodies heaving in time.

Afterward, they lay together for a long while, neither ready to move and acknowledge an ending. "My dearest," he whispered in her ear. "No woman ever has—ever will—move me as you have."

"Then you have forgiven me, my lord, for my behavior this weekend?"

He laughed softly. "How could I not, when you apologize so sweetly? But, in truth, I understood all and blamed you for little other than thwarting my plan to get you off more easily."

"But you knew why I did so?"

"Aye. I understood. And I am grateful for it, as well, though I would not have asked for it and did not truly want it."

"You should have, my lord."

"Nay." He was quiet for a moment as though he sought words to explain his feelings. "True justice knows when discipline should be tempered with mercy. This was such a case. I want to believe true justice holds more claim on me than a need to impress a family I seek to join."

"I understood that as well," she answered. "But, Jeoffrey, I wanted, nay, I needed to do that for you. You have given me so much, my very life, in truth, and a reasonable chance for a content future. I nearly cost you your future. I would have done much more to rescue what I could."

He rolled aside to lay next to her, but he pulled her close so that her head rested on his shoulder and he could stroke her hair. "Rosalind." Emotion almost overwhelmed him as she spoke. She stared upward and saw tears in his brilliant gray eyes.

"You are the most remarkable woman I have every known. My only true love and soul of my soul." He stopped and held her close, so tightly she knew he wanted never to let her go. "Yet I fear this will be our last night together. Tomorrow I go to the king and from there I rendezvous with the others for battle. Should that end satisfactorily, I have promised the duke to conclude the terms of betrothal immediately thereafter. At that time I will need an answer from you regarding which suit you choose to accept. Our futures must proceed in different paths."

"Before I go, though, I would spend this night with you. Our last together. But know that my heart will be ever in your keeping, though we never see each other again hereafter."

Chapter Nineteen

They ate a quiet but sumptuous dinner alone together in her quarters, talked for a while about how he thought the battle might be conducted, then they took to the bed again, made love, quietly and sweetly, with sad yearning, and finally slept in each other's arms.

They roused at first light. He kissed her, long and hard. When she moved to get up with him, he pressed her back on the bed.

"This is the picture I would carry with me ever in my mind. How beautiful you are in the morning, with your hair rumpled and spread over the pillow, your lovely eyes hazy with sleep and deep loving. Sad but with a loving smile on your face. Will you give me that gift?"

She nodded and somehow summoned a smile, although in truth, she felt close to breaking into tears. Still, she held the smile and put into it all she felt for him: her respect, honor, adoration, and her love.

He returned it with one of his own, leaving her with a vision of him standing tall and straight, blond hair falling around his strong, handsome face, smiling at her though she was sure she detected the shine of a tear in his gray eyes. He moved then, turning for the door but stopping for one last glance at her, and for a moment he was silhouetted against the light coming through the window: a tall man, shoulders braced to carry a burden, muscles tensed and alert. A warrior preparing for battle, for an unknown future. Alone and strong, ready to bear with grace whatever fate granted him.

And then he was gone.

She got down on her knees and prayed for the success of his mission, for his safety and that of all those accompanying him into battle, for the overthrow of Sir William and the end of his evil ambition, and for Jeoffrey's future, that whatever it held, he might find some measure of peace and happiness. Though she thought it selfish to pray for her own desires, she nonetheless threw in a request she, too, might find her way to some level of contentment.

Then she dressed hastily, climbed to the top of one of the staircases leading to the battlements, and went out. Others were there already, waiting to watch their lord and his men depart. Moments after she arrived, he rode out, dressed now in bright armor from head to foot. It gleamed in the morning sun, lending him the look of a being from beyond. The glints shooting from their mail dazzled her eyes. Two dozen knights accompanied him. She thought the one on Jeoffrey's immediate right might be Sir Philip, but she couldn't know for a certainty.

They rode off to the southwest and all too soon disappeared into the distance.

The next two weeks included some of the longest days of her life. She'd thought the endless, empty time in Sir William de Railles' dungeon had been interminable, but as she waited and wondered what was happening to Jeoffrey and the others, she found an agony clawing at her gut she couldn't ignore.

Fortunately there was plenty to do around the manor, cleaning up after the guests, putting everything back in order, replacing broken items, renewing supplies, catching up on the manor's paperwork. Since Jeoffrey had left her in charge of the manor's affairs in his absence, she took care to ensure all was kept in order. Sometimes the work helped deflect her thoughts away from the images of battle and the dread possibility Jeoffrey might be wounded or killed. Even though she knew he would never again be hers as he'd been for their eight brief weeks together, she would feel happier about her world knowing he lived in it.

Speculation, of course, was one of the chief topics of conversation in the manor, with most of the staff vowing their lord couldn't possibly fail since he was the strongest, noblest, most valiant and stalwart man any of them knew. Their loyalty was heartwarming but did little to relieve her anxiety.

They reviewed Jeoffrey's entire life, from the moment of his birth, through his childhood until he was sent off to be fostered, his occasional return visits home, and finally his taking up residence again following his father's death. Anecdotes were shared: pranks he'd pulled as a youngster, ways he'd shown his concern for others, clever things he'd said, scrapes he'd gotten into, and the beatings he'd received from his father in payment of them. They painted a vivid picture of the bright, strong, adventurous child he'd been and foreshadowed somewhat the more restrained and cautious man he'd become.

In conversation with them, she shared information and anecdotes of her own upbringing, and found in doing so, remembering the joyful times helped soften the sharpest pain of the loss of her family. The entire staff of the manor treated her now with friendliness mixed with respect, the respect they'd have offered their lady.

In other ways they deferred to her as the lady of the manor as well, waiting on her to signal the beginning of meals, consulting with her over supplies and purchases, bringing disputes to her for resolution, and on one memorable occasion, calling upon her to hear a petition for redress. Though she attempted to put off dealing with that situation, suggesting it would be more fitting to await their lord's return, Elspeth, Ferris and Chrestien all protested it shouldn't be allowed to wait and insisted she consider and render judgment on the issue.

As she listened to the complaint against one of the assistant grooms for initiating a fight with another young man that had left the latter with a black eye, bleeding nose, and a bump on his head, she understood why Jeoffrey hated this part of his responsibility. She questioned as many people as she could, sought out opinions on the character of the accused young man, and asked both participants for their versions of the incident. It required a significant weighing of evidence on her part, since the two told very different stories, a balancing of the facts she knew against their stories and what she learned of their characters. In the end she had to decide for the boy's guilt, though not without some agonizing and misgivings over whether she judged truly.

Those doubts tormented her even more when she ordered the boy to receive a dozen strokes with the strap. He took it badly, protesting his innocence and resisting getting down on the bench. Rosalind walked over to his side, put a hand on his arm, and said, so quietly only he could hear, "I hope I have made no mistake in this, but justice must be served, and you will be much more admired at its conclusion, do you conduct yourself with a man's courage and dignity now."

The young man glared at her, but nodded sharply and took his punishment with no further complaint or protest. When it was concluded and Chrestien had restored his clothes and reached down to raise him from the bench, Rosalind again moved to his side. She leaned forward to kiss him on the forehead and proclaimed as loudly as she could the incident was closed and would not be mentioned again. The boy's angry glare softened and shifted to puzzlement as he watched her. Then he turned and left the room, back held straight, eyes hard.

As the week of Lord Jeoffrey's absence stretched to a fortnight, everyone grew edgy and worried. Each time the sentries reported the approach of a newcomer on the road, excitement surged and folks gathered to greet the callers in hopes their lord returned. Three times though, the visitor proved a tradesman come to deliver supplies or a wandering tinkerer.

Nerves were stretched and the tension near to unbearable by the time an approaching cloud of dust resolved into the shape of a man clad in dusty, dented armor. Word went round the manor quickly. Anyone who could get free of his or her work assembled in the courtyard with Rosalind to greet their returning lord.

But the man who galloped in and was helped down from a tired mount wasn't Jeoffrey. It was Sir Philip.

He removed his helm and looked at the worried faces surrounding him, eyes dark and face grim. A bruise swelled at his jaw and he moved stiffly, suggesting other injuries not visible beneath his armor and clothing.

But when he found Rosalind, he bowed as well as he could and his face broke into a smile. "My lady, I rejoice to find you well."

She curtseyed in return. "And I am relieved you return to us whole as well, Sir Philip. But, pray, what news? How fares the battle? And my lord?" She knew all heard the agony in her voice on the last question.

His smile grew broader. "Worry not, my lady. The battle is won, Sir William is dead, and Lord Jeoffrey is off to the king to inform him of our victory and reaffirm his allegiance."

Cheers broke out among the throng, turning into wild hoots of joy and celebration. People clapped each other on the back, jumped up and down, yelled, and a few broke out into exuberant dances.

Relief made her knees go weak and breath come shallowly. "I thank the Lord for it," she said sincerely. Then seeing Philip sway with exhaustion, she added, "Come within, Sir Philip, and let us refresh you. What need you most immediately? Food, drink, a bath or sleep?"

"All of those, lady," he said, with a laugh. "Food and drink, first, then the bath, followed quickly by sleep. Assuming I can keep my head up through the others."

Several would-be squires gathered and assisted Sir Philip in removing his armor, then he followed her inside to the great hall, where alert servants were already bringing out wine and food for him. He moved slowly, without the quick, lithe grace she'd become used to in him, and she wondered what injuries he'd sustained and whether they required attention.

"No major wounds," he answered when she inquired about it. "A cut in my side has already been stitched and begins to heal. The rest be just the normal bumps and aches attendant on battle. Though, in truth, it was but a short, unequal battle."

"How so?" Rosalind asked. "I know from my own experience Railles was well fortified and had a sizeable force of men to defend it."

"Aye, but a significant portion of his army was away from the fortress, taking Oswood at the time. The remaining force numbered just enough to give us good contest for a short time before being overwhelmed. Jeoff himself sought out Sir William and crossed swords with him. Again the contest was barely equal, more equal than it might have been as Jeoff wore heavy armor and William only his leathers. The extra weight negated some of Jeoff's advantage of quickness. Still, he prevailed and Sir William will trouble no one further."

"The Lord be praised," Rosalind intoned. "But Oswood? How fare they?"

His laugh held real amusement. "I see the hand of the Lord in this affair, in truth," Philip said. "The bulk of Oswood's fighting force was, of course, with Jeoff, taking Railles, so the remaining inhabitants surrendered without a fight. Lord and lady and those close to them hid in some secret hole prepared for the purpose, and evidently the conquering force found them not and presumed them fled. They dared not vent their frustration on the household staff Sir William might yet need it, so they returned to Railles. Where, of course, they found us just settling in to wait for them. That battle, too, was brief and concluded satisfactorily."

"My Lord Jeoffrey is uninjured?"

"Save a few bumps and thumps similar to my own, he is quite well."

She thanked God silently this time. "And when might we expect his return?"

"He has likely already concluded his initial business with the king by now and proceeded to Barnston. I believe you know his purpose there. From thence, he will return to Court, where I am to meet him again, to finalize all the business attendant on the change of power. When all is concluded satisfactorily, he will return here. He sent me to bring you this notice now, though, to spare you further worry on his behalf."

Rosalind nodded and folded the little hope she'd retained into a secret recess of her mind where it must stay ever hidden. From the time Jeoffrey had left, she'd avoided considering the question of whose suit to accept, but now she must think on it and make her choice.

Once Philip had finished his meal, she accompanied him to his own chambers, where a bath had been prepared. To his surprise she stayed to assist him, rendering him the honor of a valued guest to be bathed by the lady of the manor. She turned away while he stripped off the rough shirt and breeches he'd worn under his armor, waiting for the betraying slosh of the water as he climbed into the tub, before she came to him.

While running the soapy cloth over his chest, face and arms, she couldn't help but be reminded of her times assisting Jeoffrey in this way. Philip was a fine-looking man himself, with broad shoulders, a lean but strong body, and regular features. Not as handsome as Jeoffrey, of course. And in truth, though she admired Sir Philip's looks, she remained unmoved by them.

But more importantly, he was a fine man in every other way—strong, honorable and good-hearted. He'd been a good friend to her. Had she met him before she'd grown to love Jeoffrey, well, who knew...

He saw her expression and took her wrist in his hand as she ran the cloth down an arm. "Lady Rosalind, if this causes you pain, pray feel no obligation to continue."

She stared at him, surprised she'd allowed her feelings to show so openly. "Nay, Sir Philip, I apologize. 'Tis an honor to assist you."

"And you cannot help but wish I were Jeoffrey." He sat up straighter and moved his hand down along her arm to take her fingers in his. "Did Jeoff tell you I had offered suit for you myself?"

She nodded. "He did and I am honored beyond words." She looked into Philip's dark, deep blue eyes. "But I fear I must decline your generous offer. I hold you in too much esteem to accept your suit."

"How so, my lady?"

"Sir Philip, you are, without doubt, one of the finest men I know. And you deserve better than a wife whose heart will ever be given elsewhere."

"I could yet end with far worse than that. In you, at least, I would know I had a lady whose honor, loyalty, integrity, and intelligence I could depend on. And we have already an understanding and friendship not be discounted. You are also quite a beautiful lady as well, and there is compensation in that."

She thought about it. "'Tis true, yet I cannot but believe that somewhere, sometime you will meet a lady who will feel about you the way I feel about Jeoffrey. I would not have you constrained in the same way Jeoffrey is now, tied by obligation to one lady while your heart yearns for another."

"I share not your confidence in the likelihood of there being another lady of beauty, honor and accomplishment equal to yours in this land. And were there, that she should honor the likes of me with her love seems unlikely."

"I disagree heartily, Sir Philip. There are many ladies more virtuous and beautiful than I around, and I should think it the likeliest thing in the world one would learn to love you."

He sighed and shook his head. "I say again I cannot share your confidence in this. Yet I see you have decided in your mind already and I will honor your wishes. Would you honor me with your plans?"

She wiped fresh soap on the cloth before she started on his hair. "Lord Michel de Granfel has offered for me, among others, but it is his suit I shall accept."

"de Granfel?" Philip almost stood up in the tub but remembered himself at the last moment and sank back into the soapy water. "He is old enough to be your grandfather."

"Aye. But I can be a comfort to his remaining years and find myself a sedate but reasonably well-portioned widow someday."

He gave her a troubled frown. "This from the lady who warns me not to settle for less than one who will love me whole-heartedly.?

"The situations are not comparable. Sir Michel knows what he can expect to get in any bargain for me, and I shall be clear what I expect settled on me in return."

Philip lay back against the side of the tub, relaxing as she massaged his scalp with soothing strokes. She knew from his frown, he wasn't pleased about her course, and knew also he wouldn't impede her since it was what she chose. Before she was done with rinsing his hair, the knight was all but asleep. She finished quickly and left him to dry himself and commit to bed.

The next morning, Philip was up at first light and prepared to depart. Rosalind thanked him for bringing them the glad news of Lord Jeoffrey's victory and requested that he send back word as soon as they knew when they planned to return to Blaisdell. Philip promised to do so.

Three days passed with no message or indication of what Lord Jeoffrey did. Though heartened by the knowledge of victory and rejoicing that the threat of Sir William no longer hung over them, she began to grow anxious again, awaiting word of Lord Jeoffrey's return. Though she knew he would come with his betrothal to Lady Alys accomplished, yet did she long to see him again. In her heart, her own decision had been made and she was, finally, at some peace with it.

On the fourth day, the awaited messenger appeared, but came in a form completely unexpected. A carriage bearing no crest or other device rumbled up to the gates and entered the courtyard. On learning she was Lady Rosalind, the driver handed her a message, which proved to be a summons to her former home, Highwaith. The note was signed by the Earl of Highwaith.

Rosalind was stunned. The king had apparently wasted no time in appointing a new earl, since no male members of her family survived to claim the estate. She hoped this new earl would be a man of comparable stature to her father, one who would do honor to the position and treat fairly with his vassals and dependents. She speculated on his reasons for summoning her, but they weren't difficult to find. No doubt he'd want to verify an accounting of the estates from whatever paperwork had survived Sir William's control. And there were features of the place only she would know: the location of a hidden safehold for valuables, among other things.

She hoped he would prove generous in his newfound grandeur. She cared about the people there and prayed for their peace and safety. And there were a few personal items still at her former home she would like to be allowed to keep.

The next morning her trunk was loaded on top of the carriage, and she rode to Highwaith for the first time since Sir William's invasion had destroyed her former life so completely. The conveyance rolled through fields, woods, and villages on its way. By midmorning she began to recognize some of the places they passed. They reached Highwaith an hour or so past midday.

Rosalind couldn't hold back a tear as the carriage approached the front entrance of the only home she'd known for her first eighteen years of life and rolled into its courtyard. Already work had begun to repair the damage done by Sir William's troops in taking the place. She regarded that as a good omen.

It stopped and the door opened. For a moment she couldn't move. She dreaded having to enter the manor and face the emptiness left by her family's deaths. Then a familiar voice inquired, "Lady Rosalind?"

"Thomas!" She jumped up and out of the carriage, throwing herself into the arms of a very surprised steward. "Thomas, you survived. I am so glad to see you again."

"And I you, my lady," the steward said. "We despaired of you along with the others. Are you well? You look lovelier than ever." He moved back and she saw tears shining in her eyes. "Come, now, my lady, no need for sadness. Come in and meet the new earl."

She hesitated. "What think you of him, Thomas? Does he seem a fair and honorable man?"

"My lady, the new earl arrived no more than three days past. We have had little time to form an opinion. But from the little we have seen… Aye, I believe he will do. Not that anyone could replace your father, or the lord your brother should have been had he survived. But his lordship… the impression of most so far is favorable."

She walked with him inside. Her heart stung as she noted the damage done to her erstwhile home by the invasion. Some of her mother's beautiful tapestries had been slashed, others torn down completely. Walls bore holes and bare spots they hadn't before and much of the loveliest furniture was missing. Many pieces had been smashed in the fighting. Others had likely been carried off. At least the place had been cleaned up and the wreckage removed. With work and expense, it could be restored to something of what it was.

"This way, my lady," Thomas said, waking her from the reverie of memories.

He knocked on the door of the room that had served as her father's place of business, then pushed it open, and said, "My lord, the Lady Rosalind."

Since the desk was in a far corner, she couldn't see the person within until she'd stepped inside. She stopped there, held motionless by shock.

"My lord… Jeoffrey!"

He stood and gave her a careful smile. "Aye, Rosalind. Sir William's ambitions were becoming a concern to the crown. The king was grateful for his removal and inclined to acknowledge himself indebted for it. I was surprised, I admit, when he named me Earl of Highwaith. I sought no such honor, and particularly not this one. Yet one says not "nay" to the king when he offers such a thing."

"Jeoffrey. Surprise alone made me exclaim as I did." She took a few steps into the room until she could see him better. "It would be a shock to confront any man in the title my father once held. Yet of all the men it might have been disposed upon, I can think of no better choice."

"My gratitude," he said. "There be a great many matters I have yet to sort out." He walked toward her and stopped a few steps away.

He looked wonderful, a dark swelling on his temple the only obvious sign of his recent battle. She wanted to touch him, to reassure herself he was real, but she dared not.

"I shall give whatever assistance is in my power," she offered.

"My thanks, my lady," he said. "I shall avail myself of your help immediately."

She couldn't bear to look at him without tears forming, so she turned and took a step toward the window.

"There is much to do here to restore it to its former grander and many things to be sorted. Yet there is one matter I would have settled forthwith," he continued. "As a new earl, I am in need of a countess."

At his last words, she froze in place, unwilling to believe she'd heard him correctly. "My lord? Did you not have an arrangement with the Duke of Barnston?"

"We encountered an insurmountable difficulty in the negotiations for the betrothal."

"An insurmountable difficulty? What could that be, my lord?"

"After seeing how I run my household, particularly the manner in which discipline is imposed, the Lady Alys wished to insert a provision into the betrothal agreement, exempting her completely and entirely from being subject to that discipline. I could not, of course, allow such an exemption. It became a point of controversy, and in the end we could reach no agreement."

In her heart, the dormant spark of hope flared into life. She tried to tamp it down, unwilling to risk the crushing disappointment should she let it flame only to find it abruptly doused. "Did the duke not protest the failure? He had already committed his forces to your effort. He made no demand you accept the provision in repayment?"

"The duke stood with my position and agreed such an exemption would not only be unprecedented in tradition, but unwise in this case. When we failed to convince the Lady Alys to drop her demand, we agreed the betrothal could not go forward. The duke was understandably disappointed, but he acknowledged no fault should accrue to me for the failure. He would not defy his daughter's will and enforce a betrothal agreement not to her liking. I cannot say I admire his reasoning. Nor yet can I regret the betrothal was not to be."

"Which leaves the question of a betrothal open," she said.

"Aye, but I find the last few months have shown me a void in my life that can be filled only by a very special lady of honor and dignity, courage and intelligence, sweetness, joy, humility, and boldness in defense of what she believes right. Know you where I might find such a one, Lady Rosalind?"

She turned to him, eyes burning with tears that threatened to spill over. "Is the absence of a dower or powerful alliances yet an issue, my lord?"

"My circumstances are much changed now, my lady. I believe I no longer need look to my bride to enhance my resources."

"Then I do believe—" She could contain the tears no longer. "Jeoffrey?" she asked, the name a plea and a promise together.

He was there at her side, wrapping her in strong arms, pulling her against his body. "Rosalind." He breathed the word into her hair. "My heart, my soul, my life. Can you bear to be the Countess of Highwaith?"

"My lord, Earl of Highwaith, Lord Jeoffrey Blaisdell, or just Jeoffrey—you alone are all I will ever want. The title mattered only for providing us the means to be together. I believe my father, could he be here today, would entirely approve of you as his successor."

He kissed her, starting at the top of her head, working down across temple and cheek until he fastened on her mouth. He kissed her until they both grew wobbly with desire. He pulled back with difficulty. "Will your family's staff be entirely shocked should we retreat to the lord's solar together and not emerge until sometime tomorrow?"

"Entirely shocked, my lord," she admitted. "And quite overjoyed, I should imagine."

"Then let us, by all means, give them joy," he said.

Epilogue

The wedding feast had been organized somewhat hastily, but was sumptuous nonetheless. Long tables groaned under the weight of roasts of fowl, pork, and beef accompanied by bowls of fresh greens, fruits, and vegetables, along with fragrant breads, custards, and cakes. Wine, ale, and fruit beverages flowed freely.

Few guests remarked on the speed of the preparations. Most were overjoyed that such an event—hoped for, but doubted—would come to pass. Lord and Lady were both radiant. Some did notice that the new countess's waist seemed not so slender as it had been, while others professed to see the omens of increase in her face. Yet none doubted the marriage owed more to the deep love of the two for each other than to any sort of expediency.

Two households mingled and quarreled in the chaos of preparation, yet in the end more friendships were born than adversaries. Jeoffrey had already announced his intention to settle at Highwaith. The inhabitants of Blaisdell voiced some disappointment, yet they understood his reasons. Their lord had already appointed a man to serve as overseer for him in his absence.

Following a moving ceremony in the church, music, dancing, eating and drinking continued until the early hours of the morning. At that late hour, a merry party accompanied the earl and his new countess to their solar to prepare them for bed.

On the way, the countess found herself beside Sir Philip. He took her hand and smiled down at her.

"Sometimes our prayers are answered and miracles truly do occur," he remarked.

"Aye," she answered. "For a long time I dreamed not this could be possible."

"I truly rejoice to see you both so happy," he said.

"I thank you, Sir Philip. Or should I say Lord Philip now? When leave you for your new manor?"

"In the morning. I'll miss your company. And Jeoffrey's."

"And we, yours, my lord. But you know we wish you all the best. And still do I believe the lady exists somewhere, perhaps even in your new manor, who will give you her heart and take yours into her keeping. She will be a very fortunate lady, indeed."

"You flatter me, Lady Rosalind," Philip said. "Yet shall I hope you are as prescient in this as you have been in the matter of your alliance with Jeoffrey."

"It will be my wish and my prayer for you."

They arrived at the solar and had no time for further conversation. The ladies helped Rosalind change to a specially prepared and embroidered nightrail, then accompanied her to meet her new lord. He, too, wore a fresh nightrail of bleached muslin.

Fragrant petals of rose, lavender, and daisy lay in drifts over the quilted bedcover. Many floated to the floor when the covers were turned back and the lord and lady tucked into their bed. Bawdy jokes and laughter flew nearly as freely, and a cheer broke out when the lord, without waiting for his guests to depart, drew his lady into his embrace and kissed her deeply.

"Out!" he ordered when a few well-wishers seemed inclined to linger.

They departed and closed the door behind them. None dared remain nearby, so none were there to hear the prolonged squeals and moans that emanated from behind the door, nor the final exultant and joyous scream that came almost simultaneously with a deeper roar of satisfaction.

When roused the next morning to attend on Lord Philip's departure, both lord and lady appeared tired, as though sleep had been little part of the night's activities, yet were they radiant in their newfound joy and the promise of the future.

BINDING PASSION

Katherine Kingston

Preview

**Available in eBook from Ellora's Cave
Publishing, Inc.
www.ellorascave.com**

Chapter One

England, 1345

Sir Philip de MontCharles, newly created Baron of Alderwood, stalked down the corridor of his manor, hoping he'd remember which door led to his private solar. He was pretty sure it was the fourth door on the left, but after only two weeks as lord of this confusing keep, he still had doubts.

He had doubts about any number of things, including his fitness to be lord of a keep, with people depending on him, their very lives possibly resting on the decisions he made. As the third son of a vigorous father, he hadn't been raised to the position.

His questions about whether he had the right room grew when he reached the door and heard a strange scrabbling, squeaking noise inside the room. Perhaps the maid was in there cleaning, but late afternoon was not, in his experience, the usual time for it. He'd always had to ask specifically for a bath to be brought to him, and he hadn't yet done so today, so he doubted that was the answer.

Given the numerous attempts already made to injure or harass him, no doubt with the object of driving him away, caution was becoming a familiar course to him.

He halted at the door and waited. Another squeak was followed by the sound of feet moving across the floor. He was pretty sure this was the door to his solar.

He wore soft indoor slippers rather than boots, so he had moved quietly down the stone-flagged hall. Whoever was inside likely hadn't heard him approach. He grabbed the door latch and pressed down on it carefully, releasing the catch without a revealing clatter. Quiet voices sounded. A small giggle followed another noise that sounded oddly like—the croak of a frog?

It all stopped abruptly when he pushed the door sharply inward. The panel swung on its hinges all the way back until it banged loudly against the wall. Two faces turned toward him, twin mirrors of surprise and guilt.

Though both were still beardless, neither of the two boys staring at him with guilty frowns was a child. For a moment, they just stood there, frozen in place by shock. A bucket behind them emitted another croak, and Philip drew the obvious conclusions.

The taller one recovered more quickly and tried to dart past Philip for the door. Philip sidestepped to block his way, and the other came at him as well. Philip hadn't spent years training as a knight to be defeated by two beardless boys in unarmed combat. The struggle was brief, the outcome inevitable.

With the two boys in neck-locks, one wedged under either arm, Philip used his foot to kick the door closed. He reached for the cord without releasing either one and pulled on it to summon a servant. He walked them over to his bed and dumped both boys onto it.

Anger and satisfaction settled in his gut as he stared at them.

"So, finally, I've caught my tormentors," he said, softly, watching them blanch as they heard the menace in his tone. "In the act. What was it to be this time?" he asked them.

"My-my lord," the taller one, whom he took to be the older as well, though he hadn't even a bit of fuzz on his face as yet, squeaked. His voice cracked. "We were here to swab the floor for you."

At that moment the bucket emitted a series of unhappy croaks, drawing all eyes toward it.

"And that's the water bucket?" he asked. "I suppose it's purely a coincidence it's making those noises." He shook his head at the boys. "Frogs in my bed this time?" he asked. "'Tis not as dangerous as some of the tricks you two have played, but 'twould certainly put me out should I have discovered myself sharing the bed with them in the late hours."

"My lord, we didn't…that is, we wouldn't…"

Philip stared hard at them. The younger one, a pale boy with brown hair and brown eyes, cringed and appeared too terrified even to speak. The older boy had lighter brown hair, lightly tanned skin, and strange, pale green eyes flecked with bronze. Those eyes met his gaze more boldly although Philip could read the fear in them as well.

"Don't compound your guilt with lies," he warned. "You're not"

A knock at the door interrupted the lecture. At his bidding a servant entered. The man's eyes widened as he took in the scene, but he wisely said only, "My lord?"

"Summon Sir Thomas, Sir Peter, and Derwyn. Tell them I have need of them in my solar immediately."

"Very good, my lord." The man made a hasty exit, shutting the door again as he left.

Philip continued to watch the two boys, though it was mostly the older one who held his attention. The younger was too frightened and timid to be much use. "While we wait, may I ask exactly what you hoped to accomplish with these…harassments?"

"We didn't…"

"Do not lie to me!" Philip's tone held an intended harshness.

Both boys flinched. The older one drew a deep breath. "What plan you to do with us, my lord?"

Philip studied them. He'd been asking himself that same question, but he knew what had to be done. "Make an example of you," he answered. He hadn't thought either one could get any paler, but both did. The younger one moaned and started to cry quietly.

The older boy leaned over and brushed a hand across his shoulder. "My lord," he said, his voice carefully controlled, "Ross was only involved in this because I made him help me." He patted the younger boy's shoulder again. "Spare him, if you please. The guilt is entirely mine."

"Admirable," Philip said, holding the older boy's gaze. "What is your name, young man?"

"Martin, my lord," the boy's voice broke into a squeak that he controlled with some effort. "Martin Fisher."

"Martin Fisher, you admit this prank was your idea and your doing? And all the other pranks as well?"

The boy nodded quickly.

"Very well. I'll keep that in mind. But your friend Ross did assist you and so cannot be entirely excused from punishment."

"But you will spare his life?"

"Spare his life?" Philip couldn't help his astonishment. "What think you I plan to do?"

"My lord, you said you'd make an example of us."

"And what do you take that to mean?"

Martin had to draw a deep breath and steady himself to speak. "A stretched neck, I should suppose." He tried to make the words light, as though he cared little about it, and failed completely.

Philip had to control a small gasp of shock on his own part. "It's past time all in this keep understood I am their lord now, whether it pleases them or no, and I shall have order and discipline in my household. That said, though," he continued, watching the boys' reactions, "I'm no tyrant either. While some of your pranks of the last few days have come close to being attempts to kill me, I would still decline to execute children for such. I think a sound whipping, performed before the assembled household, will get my point across, just as effectively."

About the author:

Katherine welcomes mail from readers. You can write to her c/o Ellora's Cave Publishing at 1337 Commerce Drive, Suite 13, Stow OH 44224.

Also by Katherine Kingston:

Why an electronic book?

We live in the Information Age—an exciting time in the history of human civilization in which technology rules supreme and continues to progress in leaps and bounds every minute of every hour of every day. For a multitude of reasons, more and more avid literary fans are opting to purchase e-books instead of paperbacks. The question to those not yet initiated to the world of electronic reading is simply: *why?*

1. *Price.* An electronic title at Ellora's Cave Publishing runs anywhere from 40-75% less than the cover price of the <u>exact same title</u> in paperback format. Why? Cold mathematics. It is less expensive to publish an e-book than it is to publish a paperback, so the savings are passed along to the consumer.

2. *Space.* Running out of room to house your paperback books? That is one worry you will never have with electronic novels. For a low one-time cost, you can purchase a handheld computer designed specifically for e-reading purposes. Many e-readers are larger than the average handheld, giving you plenty of screen room. Better yet, hundreds of titles can be stored within your new library—a single microchip. (Please note that Ellora's Cave does not endorse any specific brands. You can check our website at www.ellorascave.com for customer

recommendations we make available to new consumers.)

3. *Mobility.* Because your new library now consists of only a microchip, your entire cache of books can be taken with you wherever you go.

4. *Personal preferences are accounted for.* Are the words you are currently reading too small? Too large? Too…**ANNOYING**? Paperback books cannot be modified according to personal preferences, but e-books can.

5. *Innovation.* The way you read a book is not the only advancement the Information Age has gifted the literary community with. There is also the factor of what you can read. Ellora's Cave Publishing will be introducing a new line of interactive titles that are available in e-book format only.

6. *Instant gratification.* Is it the middle of the night and all the bookstores are closed? Are you tired of waiting days — sometimes weeks — for online and offline bookstores to ship the novels you bought? Ellora's Cave Publishing sells instantaneous downloads 24 hours a day, 7 days a week, 365 days a year. Our e-book delivery system is 100% automated, meaning your order is filled as soon as you pay for it.

Those are a few of the top reasons why electronic novels are displacing paperbacks for many an avid reader. As always, Ellora's Cave Publishing welcomes your questions and comments. We invite you to email us at service@ellorascave.com or write to us directly at: 1337 Commerce Drive, Suite 13, Stow OH 44224.

Printed in the United States
25544LVS00005B/73-390